NIGHT GARDEN

NIGHT GARDEN

A Novel

CARRIE MULLINS

OLD COVE PRESS

LEXINGTON, KENTUCKY 2016

Published by
Old Cove Press
Lexington, Kentucky
oldcove.com

Distributed by
Ohio University Press
30 Park Place, Suite 101
Athens, Ohio 45701
ohioswallow.com

Paperback ISBN: 978-0-9675424-4-7
Electronic ISBN: 978-1-7352242-3-7

This is a work of fiction. Names, characters, businesses, places,
events, and incidents are used fictitiously, and any resemblance
to actual persons, living or dead, is entirely coincidental.

Design by Nyoka Hawkins

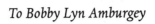

To Bobby Lyn Amburgey

PART ONE

ONE

MARIE COULD SEE THE FIRE up ahead through the trees. She could see sparks pull away from the flame and swirl up into the dark. It made her stomach tighten. She could see a hand shoot up, a shadow backlit by the flame, and she heard someone call out, long and slow, *Heeeee yeooow!* It was a yell full of the joy of being drunk on a Saturday night.

Marie, her brother Shane, and their teacher Ms. Anglin got out of the car. Marie wiped her hands on her jeans. They got the cooler and the guitar out of the trunk and started down the old logging road. They had to go around the wet mud pit in the middle of the road, had to walk up into the woods a little bit, over rocks they couldn't see for dead leaves, and then back down onto the wide path, until the shadows they'd been watching became people and they could feel the bonfire heat on their own faces.

Marie stopped counting how many of these parties she'd been to there in the woods in Larkin County. At home in Caudill, she and Shane would never be invited to a place like this, at the end of an old logging road, not with people like the Owenses. Shane didn't care, he was just putting in time with Ms. Anglin until he started college. Ms. Anglin wanted to go because they were her people, the Owenses. Nobody knew Ms. Anglin down in Larkin County except the Owenses, and they were too busy getting wild to worry about who she brought to their parties.

Shane and Marie set the cooler down in the usual place, and the usual guy took out three beers the second it hit the ground, before Marie could take her seat on it. Marie was seventeen and her job was just to be there. Keep her parents from thinking Shane was into anything wild. Keep her mouth shut about him and Ms. Anglin. Marie watched the Owenses, listened to their music about Sin City, listened to them talk. She wanted to talk with them, about camping and going four-wheeling and staying up all night. Someday she would do that, she would just go over and sit right there among them and talk with them, instead of sitting over on the cooler, watching.

They hadn't been there more than fifteen minutes when Marie caught a flash of movement from across the fire. Shane in his white T-shirt among all the gray and brown clothes of the Owenses, Ms. Anglin in her black silky kimono top. They were fighting again. Ms. Anglin pushed Shane's shoulder, then closed in on him and wouldn't let him move. Marie couldn't hear the words but she knew what it was about, same as all their other fights. Shane was going away to college, he was going to leave her, go off to Lexington and not ever look back. She just knew it, she said. They were less like fights, more like a sad clown who won't let her audience leave. Shane usually let her vent until she was ready to pass out.

Ms. Anglin was right up in his face this time though, her finger an inch from his nose. Shane looked at her for a minute then down at her finger. He moved his head back so he could get a better look at it. Then he opened his mouth and lunged. He bit down on her finger and her back arched so very slightly at the pain. She stood silent and motionless and there they were in a weird frozen pose, connected tooth to finger. Marie couldn't help but think about finding the two of them in the school darkroom Shane's sophomore year, connected then too, but at different parts of their bodies. Then the frozen picture moved and Ms. Anglin screamed and all hell broke loose around them. One of Ms. Anglin's girl cousins saw what happened and swatted at Shane, he opened his mouth and let the finger go. Ms. Anglin brought her hurt hand to her chest, cradled it with the other hand. She cussed Shane. Then she looked down at her finger. "It's bleeding!" she screamed.

Everybody at the party looked at the two of them. The Owens brothers circled around. Marie went and stood in the circle too. "What the hell?" one of the brothers asked, the one named Keith.

"You punk!" Ms. Anglin said. "You stupid punk! Come here!" She slapped Shane hard across the face. Then she hugged him. "I'm sorry," she said. And then she said, "Why did you do that?" She repeated those two things over and over, like a chant. "I'm sorry! Why did you do that?" People stood around them stiff-legged, not really sure if the fight was over.

"Shoot, Jilly, there's not even a mark on there," Keith said, leaning over her hand that was now around Shane's neck. The brothers moved away from the two of them, Ms. Anglin still with her arms around Shane and saying something in his ear, Shane looking straight ahead, his arms down by his sides.

AFTER THE FIGHT, Shane disappeared into the woods up above the fire, left with one of the Owens boys to get high. As soon as he was out of sight, Ms. Anglin put a camp chair beside Marie. She got a beer and some ice out of the cooler then sat down and showed Marie her finger. "So what's going on with him?" she asked, holding the ice on her finger. "Does he have a girlfriend?"

"I thought you were his girlfriend," Marie said. There was something about Ms. Anglin that made Marie feel sorry for her, something about the way she always needed to be reassured.

"I've seen him talking to that Miller girl," Ms. Anglin said. "I know he's screwing that Miller girl. Oh God, I love him." Marie looked down at her hands in her lap, down at the ground, looked at anything except her journalism teacher. "I'm only six years older than him. That's nothing. In the grand scheme of things, it's a drip in the bucket."

You're a drip, Marie thought.

Ms. Anglin took a long drink. "What do you think? You think I'm too old for him, don't you?" but she wouldn't let Marie answer. "Shit, twenty-four's not old, I'm not old." After a few minutes, she said, "I love him, that's all. I just love him. He almost took my finger off." She held out her finger for Marie to inspect again but Marie didn't even pretend to look at it this time. "You been in love," she said. "You know."

Marie shook her head. Ms. Anglin had to bring up Kyle. "Nope," Marie said.

Ms. Anglin got up, threw down the ice she'd been holding to her finger. "It's crazy, man. It's crazy." Then she staggered around the fire to some of her cousins.

14

MARIE SAW SHANE come down the hill and mix back into the party, which had shot to life after the finger bite, people had unloosed. Boys lost their shirts in the still-hot summer night, and girls took the ponytail holders off their wrists and put their hair up to get it off their necks. One girl fell off a hay bale. She was just sitting there and then she wasn't, she'd slumped all the way down to the ground. People gathered around to make sure she was okay. Two guys did karate on each other on the other side of the fire. Somewhere up in the darkness, above the log road in the woods, a voice yelled out *Heeelll yeeeah!*

Shane came over to Marie, got a beer from the cooler and took a gulp. He made a sour face and blew out the beer. "Hot as piss," he said, then took another gulp anyway. "She can't even get beer cold." Ms. Anglin stood across the fire from them, beside a big rock with Keith, his brother Ed, and his sister Nikki. Ms. Anglin hadn't noticed Shane was back or she would have been sitting right there between Marie and her brother.

"I can't wait to be out of here," Shane said, his eyes still on Ms. Anglin. He'd leave for Lexington the next day, move-in day for the University of Kentucky summer session.

"What about Ms. Anglin?" Marie asked.

"Hell," he said, and shook his head. He took another drink of the warm beer. "Sorority girls, that's what I'm—" He made a clicking noise with his mouth and winked.

One of the karate guys kicked the other one into the fire. He rolled out of the flames, smoke coming off of him, but nobody got excited. He jumped up and held up his hands like he'd scored a touchdown and yelled *I'm all right! I'm all right!*

"She thinks you're messing with that cheerleader," Marie said.

Shane gave her his serious look, his older brother look, like she shouldn't talk like that. All his gestures were exaggerated and slow because he was so high. "It doesn't matter," he said. "It just doesn't matter." He leaned over toward Marie so he could talk low. "Listen," he said, "it's over. *Shhh!*" He pointed at Ms. Anglin then put his finger up to his mouth. "*Shhh!* Don't tell her."

Marie was glad he told her his secret. People did that, told her secrets, she didn't know why.

"You're going to have to take care of yourself," Shane said. He leaned over and nudged her with his shoulder. "Okay?" He leaned over onto her again, a little harder this time, needing some response from her.

"I will."

"You know if it gets weird you can call me."

Marie nodded. There were a lot of things Marie and Shane didn't talk about, including their parents, but they both knew what he meant.

"Just, you know," he said.

"Yeah," she said.

WHEN THEY LEFT the party, it was almost light. They drove back down the gravel road, onto a blacktop road, then north on Highway 25. They passed the little white houses and tan trailers of Larkin County. The few houses were bunched up together along the road, probably a grandma in the older small white house, aunts and uncles and cousins in the newer houses and trailers clustered around it.

Then they drove through the town of Crawford. The town looked like it had died a long time ago, with boarded-up buildings, a pool hall with an open door and a mattress in the doorway, an auto parts store, a drugstore, a dollar store, and some lawyer offices locked up tight with bars over plate glass windows.

Ms. Anglin woke up for a second, leaned across the seat, and put her head on Shane's shoulder as he drove. "I sure am going to miss you, tadpole," she said, and fell back asleep. Shane sped up to seventy on the straight part of the highway.

When they got to Ms. Anglin's house, Shane and Marie lugged her gear from the trunk and dropped it on her front porch.

"See you," Shane said and gave a goodbye salute.

Marie stayed on the porch steps for a minute. Ms. Anglin shook her head, told Marie to call her. Shane honked the horn. Marie jumped off the steps and ran through the yard to his car, and they drove on home to Caudill.

TWO

MARIE SAT BY THE POOL at her friend Makinley's house in a blue and yellow bikini Makinley had stolen from Belk's. It wasn't that cute. Marie couldn't figure out what possessed her to take it, especially in a size that would only fit Marie. They listened to the radio. They ate cherries Makinley's mother had washed and put in a wooden bowl for them. Some kind of handcrafted bowl, because that was the kind of thing Makinley's mom appreciated.

Marie's parents' company built the Gordons' big house out in the country. It had high ceilings and wooden beams, warm wood cabinets spotlighted by recessed lighting. They built the deck too, with a stone outdoor fireplace and a redwood pergola, like the one Makinley's mother had seen in a magazine. Marie moved to the shade of the pergola because she was hung over from the night before, all those hot Budweisers she drank with Shane in Larkin County bubbled up in her stomach and made her head hurt.

The phone rang and Makinley picked it up. "It's for you." She handed the receiver to Marie. There was a hum in the phone and Marie couldn't hear very well. At first she thought it was Ms. Anglin, calling to ask about her brother, but the female voice on the other end of the line sounded like her mom. Marie sat up in her chair, delicately, for her throbbing head.

"Marie, this is your Aunt Camille," the voice said. Her aunt lived near Cincinnati, Marie hardly ever saw her. "There's been an accident, Shane and your mom were in a car accident."

Marie moved to the edge of her chair. She almost let the receiver drop out of her hands. "Your mom is okay, but Shane is in intensive care. Your dad's on his way to the hospital. Can you get a ride to Lexington?"

Makinley drove Marie to the university hospital. Marie didn't realize until much later that night that she still had the blue and yellow bikini on under her shorts and tank top.

THE FIRST TIME Marie prayed, really prayed, was in the ICU waiting room. Her brother was unconscious, hooked to a machine that breathed for him. Her mom was in another hospital room, bruised with some broken ribs but recovering. Her dad slept in a chair on the other side of the waiting room.

Marie looked at her dad. His neck was at a bad angle. His arms were across his chest, stretching his windbreaker tight across his biceps. His legs stuck straight out.

She wished she could close her eyes. The waiting room was cold and she pulled her arms inside the sweatshirt Makinley had loaned her. The other people in the waiting room were mostly sleeping. The room had yellow floor tiles like her high school cafeteria, lunchroom tables replaced by blue hospital chairs, small wooden tables stacked with magazines.

Her father shook awake. "You want something to eat?" he asked. She could tell he wasn't fully awake. His question didn't really make sense in the middle of the night. She said no and he fell back asleep. Marie looked harder at her dad this time. Shane and their mom had left for Lexington that morning with clothes and towels and bed sheets, milk crates filled with stuff he'd need at college. She was going to ride up later with their dad in the truck, they were bringing the little refrigerator and other things he'd need in his dorm. She wondered what her dad said to Shane before he drove away in his Mustang, their mom in the passenger seat. Marie wished she had been there.

She always felt cool and clear riding in her brother's car. They didn't talk much, they never talked much, they just drove. Sometimes Marie felt like a stranger in her own family, like everyone else was more perfect and more, something. She was not put together like the rest of them. Out on the road, riding with her brother, she didn't feel that way.

All they could figure was that Shane fell asleep at the wheel. Marie thought about the party around the fire the night before. She imagined him nodding off on the interstate, veering off the edge of the highway, leaving his car a twisted wad of metal at the bottom of a steep bank.

THREE

MARIE NEVER KNEW how much coffee to put in, even after she read the instructions on the blue coffee can. One tablespoon per six ounces of water. How many ounces were in a cup? She couldn't remember.

It smelled like Grandma Massey's house as the coffee brewed. She thought about her grandma's kitchen, the round oak table, the cookie jar that looked like a big purple ceramic onion. One small countertop, lemon yellow laminate with a thin edge of stainless steel, hardly enough space to roll out biscuits. The porcelain bell Marie's uncle sent with a painting of Monument Valley on it, the one they'd ring when they came in so their grandma would know they were there in her kitchen, because she cooked with her hearing aid off. Marie thought about how her grandma's garden went to seed after she died last summer, tomatoes rotted on the vine, squash turned to mush on the ground, the weeds overtook all she had planted in the spring.

Marie started on the biscuits, pouring the flour into the bowl, making the well in it like she learned in home economics class, using a fork to mash the butter into the flour. She worked at the island in the middle of the kitchen, across from the fireplace and the upholstered chairs her mom had seen in a model home somewhere. The marble on the island was so cold that when she touched it, it made her shiver.

She was making breakfast for supper, Shane's favorite. She wanted to finish everything before her parents got home. She opened the stainless steel refrigerator and got out the sausage, sliced it, put the pink circles in a skillet and turned on the gas range. She put the eggs in a bowl and added milk and pepper and salt. She set the breakfast bar for three people leaving the chair closest to the window alone, with only the placemat there, no plate or silverware or coffee mug.

In the weeks since the wreck Marie never knew what to do with herself when she was at home. Didn't know where to put her hands. Didn't know where to sit. When her mom was around, Marie avoided anything Shane had ever touched. Her mom made shrines throughout the house, his chair at the breakfast bar, his room, his books, his shoes, his T-shirts. Her dad had grown a beard. And he had sort of grown into the couch, where he stayed all the time when he was home. He hardly moved and wouldn't even change the TV channel. For hours at a time the television would stay on QVC, her father staring blankly at women selling jewelry and cosmetics.

But neither of her parents were there yet so Marie sat where she wanted, in the seat without a plate, while the supper cooked. When she heard the door slam, she jumped up and went back to the stovetop. Her mom threw her purse onto the counter. "Have you seen your father?" She was wearing her diamond stud earrings and a sweater with *Massey Construction* embroidered on the front.

"No."

Her mom closed her eyes, put her hands on the counter. "Has he called?" She checked the answering machine. No messages. She walked back to the island and sat down heavily on a barstool. "He's gone again."

Marie moved closer, but stayed across the island from her mother. "He didn't come to the office," her mom said. "He wasn't at the site today. I just don't know." Marie didn't know either, and she didn't know what to say. It was the third time since the funeral her dad had disappeared.

"Did you try the golf course?" That was where they found him last time, sitting in his golf cart in the cart barn, doing nothing, just sitting there in his work clothes and boots.

"Yes, I tried the golf course!" Her mom was almost shouting. Then softer, she said, "He thinks he's the only one who lost anything." She started crying.

"I made some biscuits, and sausage, and coffee," Marie said. "How about some coffee?" She turned away from her mom and went to the coffee maker. She got a mug and poured it not quite full, leaving room for lots of milk, just the way her mom liked it. "Here," Marie said, and put the coffee where she could reach it, if she wanted to.

She came around behind her mom and started rubbing her back. She followed the same path, shoulder to shoulder, then down her back, following the triangle shape of her upper body, crossing over bony spine again and again, hoping she would stop crying and eat supper.

"I need him now the most and he's gone," her mom said. "I can't do this by myself."

"I know." It was all Marie could think to say. Her mom got up and walked to the bathroom in the foyer.

Marie scrambled some of the eggs, took the biscuits out of the oven, and put the sausage on a plate. She cut up an orange and got some grapes out of the refrigerator. She made a plate for her mom and set it in her usual place.

Her mom finally came out and sat down. Marie looked at her. Her makeup had worn off but she was still beautiful, with perfect bones, straight white teeth. She looked down at her plate and shook her head. "I don't even know where to look for him."

MARIE REMEMBERED when her mother signed her up for the Miss Hawkins County Pageant, the summer after freshman year. "This is something we can do together," her mom said. After two weeks of trying on dresses and practicing walking, Marie wasn't so sure they were doing it together. Her mom bought her a suit for the interview when Marie wasn't even at the store. "It was on sale at Belk's," she told Marie. It was purple, with a windowpane check, gold buttons, skirt to the knee. It was also too big, and Grandma Massey agreed to take it in.

"So what is this for?" her grandma asked, as she pinned the jacket at the seams around Marie's waist. Shane had driven Marie to their grandma's house, and her hearing aid was whistling because the battery was low.

Marie hesitated, looked over at Shane who was watching golf on TV. "It's for a pageant, Grandma, I'm going to be in a beauty pageant." Marie yelled so that she could hear.

"All right, take off the jacket now." Her grandma took the jacket into the bedroom where her sewing machine was set up.

Marie sat down in the love seat and watched golf with Shane. When her grandma came back in, she helped Marie put the jacket on. She turned her around. "Looks all right," she said. "I guess that's what she wanted done." She leaned down and pulled on the bottom of the skirt, stood back up and looked at the whole outfit. "I don't know about all this, beauty pageant is nothing but a parade of half-naked girls, seems to me. Ought not throw your pearls before swine." Shane looked at her. He and their mom didn't like Grandma Massey, with her faded housedresses and dollar store shoes.

Marie wasn't exactly sure what she was talking about, pearls before swine, but Marie guessed she was the pearl. She couldn't figure who the swine was.

"Mom did it when she was my age."

Her grandma made Marie turn around again. "And it seems a waste of money to me," she said.

Shane jumped up then. "She can do what she wants. She doesn't have to answer to you."

He made Marie leave the minute things were finished. They got in the car and when they got to the store where they usually stopped, Shane turned to Marie. "What I mean is you don't have to take her shit, and you don't have to take mom's shit either. Don't do the pageant crap for her. And don't not do it because the old bat doesn't think you're good enough. This all pisses me off." He got out of the car and went into the store.

Marie was pretty sure Shane didn't understand what Grandma Massey had said. He thought she didn't think Marie was good enough to be in a pageant. Marie thought her grandma thought she was too good.

He came back and handed her an extra-large lime slush. "You don't have to be in the pageant if you think it's stupid," he said, "and I get the idea you think it's stupid." Marie took a sip as he talked. "That's all I'm trying to say."

She had just wanted to make her mom happy, and it seemed like the pageant was one way to do that. Even though the thought of being onstage made her so nervous she could hardly breathe. Even though Makinley bitched that it wasn't even a scholarship pageant. It might have been the only thing she could have done, ever, that excited her mom. Shane would never be able to understand that.

In the end, Marie didn't place in the Miss Hawkins County Pageant. Neither did Makinley. Her mom told them afterward, "You all looked miserable up there, like you didn't want to be there. That's why you lost."

FOUR

M s. ANGLIN SET UP lines of Oxy for them on her coffee table. "This shit has been messing me up," she said.

She handed Marie a straw and told her to go first, so Marie did. Then she laid back on Ms. Anglin's carpet seeing trees and a forest all around, summer trees that were green and hopeful.

"See what I mean?" Ms. Anglin said. "See?"

Marie felt her take the straw from her hand, heard her suck up the second line. She could hear Ms. Anglin breathing across the room, she could hear the freezer making ice in the kitchen. She could hear even though she couldn't see anything but the trees that had grown in Ms. Anglin's living room. Marie couldn't say anything for all those trees, she wasn't able to open her mouth.

The next thing Marie knew they were in the car, Ms. Anglin careening one lane to the other, but who cared. She could drive with her elbows, it wouldn't matter. They'd get there. It was inevitable. The party by the fire and the car were moving toward each other, across time and space, they would meet and everyone would be together and Marie would be there too.

Everything made Marie laugh. Ms. Anglin's car window that wouldn't roll down. The whiny man on the CD player singing and playing guitar.

And finally the car and the party did meet in space and time and the car stopped. Marie felt herself glide out of the car and around the mud pit and down the road to the party.

MARIE WANTED to talk to everyone there. She had something to say, even to people she had never seen before. She asked the older Owens uncles about the beer they were drinking and they gave her one. She talked to Nikki Owens, Ms. Anglin's cousin she couldn't make herself talk to when she was straight, because Nikki was too cool. Nikki had on a bikini top with a leather vest over it and jeans. Marie told her she had cool clothes. "You are way fucked up," Nikki said, and Marie smiled and moved on.

Everyone at the party was talking about Bobo, the other Owens brother who'd been off working in Indiana. Everybody there talked about him like he was a superstar. He was coming home in a couple weeks. Then they'd really party.

Marie felt taller and she liked the way she felt when she walked, like her joints were jangling, like she was tall and limber, moving easy over the ground. And it felt like everyone noticed her and wanted to talk to her as much as she wanted to talk to them. Everything was happening for a reason, and she knew what the reason was, even if she couldn't say it out loud.

Nobody reminded her of anything and everybody at the party was good. The only thing missing was water. She wanted to dive

30

into a pool and swim, or a lake or a river or something. It would have felt so good to move her body around in some water, it would have made the night totally complete.

Marie ran into Ms. Anglin and she was saying, to no one, "How did we come to be here?" She was saying it over and over again, not talking to Marie or anyone else, asking God, it seemed like, with her palms up, cigarette burning in one hand, head cocked to one side. "Man, that's all I want to know. I want to know how we came to be here." She shook her head and brought the cigarette to her lips, left the other arm outstretched. "And here's the other thing I need to know—" She paused and blew out a stream of smoke. "Why is *he* not *here*?"

That pissed Marie off. She knew what Ms. Anglin was talking about, she knew *who* Ms. Anglin was talking about. "It doesn't make sense. It just doesn't even make sense," she heard Ms. Anglin say as she stumbled off. Ms. Anglin, who Shane was done with, who he was trying to get away from, was now bringing him up, when all Marie wanted to do was get away, forget about the way her mother wailed at the funeral, and the broken shell that was left of her dad. Why was she talking about this now, just when Marie had almost been able to forget what happened, even just for a few hours. Ms. Anglin ruined it.

Marie tried to shake it off. She remembered water. It was July and it was hot and she wanted to jump into some water, so she asked one of the Owens cousins if there wasn't a pool or a pond around there somewhere. He was about the same age as Marie and his name was Everett. He smiled and said, "Yeah, back over here, follow me." So she did, she followed him into the woods, and when they were far away from the party, he said, "Just a little farther, over this little rise here." But when they got over the rise, he grabbed Marie's hair and pulled it back and hurt her and she yelled out for him to stop, but he pulled her hair harder, pulled it down and told her to shut up, and then he pushed her down into the dry leaves and stood over her and unbuckled his belt. She tried to get up but he pushed her down again and was on top of her tearing at her clothes and biting her.

Then Marie heard a voice. It was Nikki in her bikini top and leather vest. She called Everett a little piss ant cocksucker and told him he better get his punk ass back to the party and get his goddamn pants pulled up or he was going to have some trouble.

"We was just—" Everett said, but Nikki told him to shut up and told him if she ever saw him pull this shit again she would personally cut his balls off. Marie heard him hurry through the woods back to the party.

Then Nikki turned to Marie, who was still on the ground. "As for you, I don't want to see your face around here either, coming in here so fucked up you can't even take care of yourself." She held out her hand to help Marie up. "Little girls and boys coming around here acting like they're big and bad. It's going to get bad for you if you keep this up, you little dumbass." She pulled a leaf out of Marie's hair. "And you can tell Jilly Anglin I said so."

She followed Nikki back to the fire. Marie was embarrassed and sick. She went to Ms. Anglin's car and locked the doors and laid down in the back seat. Later she got out of the car and laid on the car hood for a while, just looking up at the sky. The party was still going on but there weren't many people there. It felt like it was just her and the stars up in the sky. They were so clear out there, the Milky Way stretched across the blackness, clouds full of stars so far out in space, so far out that a person on earth could not even imagine the distance. All the people she had been close to might as well have been stars in the Milky Way, they were that far away from her. She closed her eyes when she felt like she was going to throw up, then rolled over and vomited down the side of Ms. Anglin's car. When she was sober enough to be scared that Everett would come back, she got back in the car and locked the doors and fell asleep in the back seat.

FIVE

Bobo owens didn't notice Marie the first night he was
home from Indiana. Probably because he had just got back and
had to talk to everybody who crowded around him, asking him
things and telling him what had happened in Crawford while he
was gone. It didn't help that Marie was just wearing jeans and a
black T-shirt, her hair all gunky and in a ponytail.

By the next party though, she was ready. She picked out a blue
tank top with a short denim skirt and flat sparkly sandals. She
brushed her hair out and put that stuff on it that made it shiny.
She went through her mom's jewelry and found a leather neck-
lace with wooden beads, something her mom must have worn
in high school. She left a note for her parents saying she was
spending the night with Makinley.

Ms. Anglin picked her up and they went to her house and got
high. They drank a couple beers on the drive to Larkin County.

Bobo's sister Nikki was the first person Marie saw at the party. Marie had steered clear of her since the scene with cousin Everett. She couldn't help but watch her though. That night Nikki wore a long dress with lace and beads sewn on it. It was peach-colored and it moved and swished when she walked. Her hair was long and straight and she looked like she walked out of a movie from the 1970s. Marie watched as Nikki moved around the party. Marie kept her distance.

When Bobo showed up, it was like he walked out of his own movie. He rolled out of his Jeep Cherokee like a star, walked on the log road like it was a red carpet. He was tall with wide straight shoulders and wore overalls and a camo hat with sunglasses on top. He was older, Marie didn't know how old, maybe thirty. She watched him move into the party. He said something to everyone there. He got around to where his brothers Keith and Ed and his sister Nikki were sitting. He smiled at Nikki and hugged her. Marie wanted to be standing there too, next to all of them. She wanted to hear what Bobo was saying, hear what they all were saying. She wanted that light that glowed around them to glow up around her too. She moved toward them, slow, watching them as she walked.

Ms. Anglin walked up and hugged Bobo, patted him on the back. Bobo sat down across from Keith. They both had a beer in their hands. Marie came up and stood next to Ms. Anglin. Somebody pulled out a joint and they passed it around. When it got to Marie, Bobo looked at her. He looked at Ms. Anglin then back at Marie. "Who's this?" he asked.

Ms. Anglin said, "That's Marie, my friend Marie."

Bobo smiled. "You from Hawkins County?"

Marie nodded and smiled back at him. He handed her a beer, motioned for her to take a seat right beside him, so she did. Keith started talking smack. "Hawkins County. Them fuckers up at Walters got some kind of mental problem. All that damn mustard gas or something. You ain't from Walters, are you?"

Marie shook her head. "Caudill."

"Ho shit, Caudill. That's no better," Keith said. "You a college girl then? You ain't no damn hippie like Jilly Anglin's turned into, are you? Listening to all that psychedelic crap at college. You ain't no damn hippie, are you? "

"Not really," Marie said.

After they had been sitting there talking for a while, Bobo closed and opened his eyes slow. Looked right at Marie. Half smiled. It made her feel warm. Made her want to be closer to him, made it hard to breathe, in a good way. Made her know she was alive, in a body sitting next to him.

Later on, Marie got cold so she went to get Ms. Anglin's denim jacket from the car. She walked away from the fire, down the road through the trees on the other side of the muddy circle.

"Hi," someone said.

She jumped a little, and turned to the voice. It was Bobo.

"Hi," she said. He had the same high cheekbones as Nikki, like polished stones. Like those polished rocks they sell in barrels down in Gatlinburg.

"What's going on back here?" he said.

Marie opened the door of the car and got the jacket, then closed it. "I'm cold," she said. The jacket was too big and smelled like perfume, no kind of perfume Marie would wear.

"So what's your deal?" Bobo asked.

Marie leaned back against the car, thought for a minute. She could hear the party, the people, and the music up by the fire. All those people who had been talking about Bobo, waiting for him to come home, telling stories about him, each story bigger and wilder than the one before. Now he was here, and he was with her, asking her what her deal was.

"My deal," she laughed. "I don't know."

"How'd you get here?"

"Ms. Anglin. You know."

"Good old Jilly," Bobo said. He moved up beside her. They both looked straight ahead, watching the people at the party, who were dark silhouettes against the fire.

"You got a boyfriend?"

"Nope." It came out too quick and Marie wished she had made him wait awhile for that answer. She sneaked a sideways look at him. Up close he was all muscle, hard and solid. She kept her palms on her skirt hoping it would soak up the sweat in case he tried to take one of her hands.

"You ever been down on the river?"

She said no.

"We'll go sometime. You ever been in a canoe?"

She said no again.

"You don't know what you been missing."

"What am I missing?" she asked, still not looking at him.

He slid closer to her. "I'll get you down there. You'll see. We'll start out on the flat water, move up from there." It was quiet for a minute. "You can swim, right?"

Marie nodded.

"Jill says you like to party." He was looking at her now.

"Yeah, I guess."

"Yeah, me too."

Then someone yelled, "Bobo!" They could see his brothers Keith and Ed, two silhouettes together, their heads thrown back and their mouths wide open. "Bobo!" They both yelled this time. "Get your ass over here!"

Bobo laughed. "Well, it looks like I've been summoned."

Marie wasn't ready for him to leave. It felt like they had just started talking.

"I'll catch you later," he said. "And you are going with us, out on the river."

"Okay."

"Good." He jogged up the logging road and joined his brothers. She watched them talk for a while. It looked like they were laughing and joking, people around them laughing and joking too. Nikki came up. Bobo put his arm around her. Marie wondered what they were saying, like brothers and a sister from a movie or something. It was a movie Marie wanted to be in.

ON THE DRIVE home, Ms. Anglin said, "Bobo thinks you're cute. He likes you."

Marie looked out the car window. Her face was so close to the window her breath fogged it up.

"Yeah," Ms. Anglin said. "He wants to take you down on the river. He wants everybody to go. Party down there."

They drove on in the darkness until they pulled into Ms. Anglin's driveway. Marie helped her drain the melted ice out of the cooler, took the few beers left and put them on the bottom shelf of the refrigerator. Ms. Anglin went to the bathroom and came out with her nightshirt on. Marie got the toothbrush from her backpack, brushed her teeth, and got under the scratchy blanket on the couch. Ms. Anglin said goodnight, turned off the lights, and went to her bedroom. Marie drifted to sleep after she thought about what it would be like to kiss Bobo Owens, to sleep with him in a tent by the river.

SIX

MARIE STEPPED OFF the sidewalk down onto the grayed asphalt of the school parking lot. She looked over toward the cars parked in the student section, and for a second she thought Shane's car would be there, she wished he would be there, sitting in his Mustang, waiting to pick her up.

When he was alive, Shane never picked her up from school, he was always busy doing something else, so it didn't make sense, but it was still there, like an ache, this longing to see him sitting in his car in the lot. She scanned every spot just to make sure.

Kids peeled out and smoke rose from their back tires, but they had to stop in the line-up behind the buses. Kyle passed her in his mother's little red car, he passed by her and didn't honk or wave. She looked for Makinley's car. She expected to ride home with her, but didn't see her car in the corner where she usually parked.

What she did see was her mother's gold SUV and her mother inside, looking right at her, both hands on the wheel even though the car was parked. Something was up. Marie tried to look away, tried to act like she didn't see her there, but her mother honked and waved, pulled out of the space and drove toward her.

The drive home was silent and heavy. Marie knew something was coming, but she wasn't sure what. Maybe her parents were going to get a divorce. Maybe her mother was moving out for good this time. When they pulled into the garage, before they got out of the car, her mother started. "I know you haven't been staying at Makinley's," she said. "We need to talk."

Marie's head dipped. It was a complete surprise, and her body couldn't hide it. Her mom put the car in park and got out, went around to Marie's side so she couldn't escape, and they walked into the house through the kitchen door.

They stopped at the kitchen counter and her mom put down her purse and keys. "I talked to Makinley's parents, Marie. You weren't there this weekend." The circles under her mom's eyes were a light purple and the lines across her forehead looked as deep as garden rows. "You haven't been staying with her the other times you said either." Marie took off her backpack and held it in her hands.

"Where were you?" Marie was silent.

"Answer me." Her mother's voice seemed to go octaves lower and got really soft. Her eyes were searching Marie's face like she could find all the answers there. "Were you with Kyle?"

"No," Marie said, so quick that her mom's head cocked to the side, eyebrow went up.

"Well, where were you then?" Marie didn't answer.

"You're just going to stand there? You and your dad think you can just abandon me, is that it?"

42

Marie wanted to leave the kitchen, but her legs wouldn't work. She closed her eyes.

"You've got to be honest with me here." Marie looked at the ceiling and then away from her mom. "And don't roll your eyes at me. Why are you rolling your eyes at me?"

Her mom sat down on a barstool. "Okay, so that's it, you're not going to tell me where you've been. All right. Go upstairs to your room, and don't come out until you're ready to talk. And don't think for a minute I won't find out, because I will. Mark that down, I will find out."

"I'm not five years old," Marie said.

"I know how old you are. And I know you're lying to me and it's going to stop."

Marie felt weird and then hot under her mother's stare. "I have some friends in Larkin County. We hang out."

Her mom took a breath in. "Larkin County? And who do you know down there?"

"They were Shane's friends, and mine." She wanted her mom to know Shane had taken her down to Larkin County, that these were his friends she was hanging out with.

"Incredible," her mom said. "After all I've been through, Marie."

Marie picked up her backpack and walked upstairs. She flopped onto her bed and didn't bother to take off her shoes.

A few days later, after Marie promised never to go to Crawford again, things at the Massey house settled back to normal. Her mom was gone every night of the week and so was her dad.

SEVEN

MARIE SPENT THE NIGHT at Ms. Anglin's. They left her house very early the next morning, drinking coffee from a couple of her travel mugs. They headed to Crawford for a trip on the river with Bobo.

Bobo's house was on a run-down street. Ms. Anglin said his great aunt left him the place. It was stucco with a detached garage. An Eagle Talon leaned toward the Jeep Cherokee in the driveway, the Talon's tires were flat on one side and dry-rotted. His brothers and their girlfriends were already there. They parked in the yard and were lashing canoes to the tops of their cars. Bobo came out the door with coffee in his hand, smiling.

"Park over there," he said to Ms. Anglin. "You all can ride with me." When they got out of the car, he motioned to Marie. "Help me out here in the garage." She followed him. One green canoe and one red canoe rested upside down on a long worktable in the back. He slid one end of the red canoe off the table and put it in Marie's hands. "Got it?" She nodded. He picked up the other end and they carried it out to the driveway, hefted it onto the roof of the Jeep, the canoe still upside down. They went back to the garage and got the green one. She watched Bobo fasten the bungee cords around the canoes and the roof rack. He came back around and patted each of the canoes, seeing if they were secure. "That'll do it," he said.

He looked through the back window at the camping gear he'd already put in. Then he snapped his fingers. "Beer!" He jogged to the house and brought out a cooler. Marie could hear the bottles clinking and the ice moving in there. He opened the back hatch and put it in with the camping gear.

His brothers smoked in the yard with their girlfriends. "You ready yet?" one of them yelled at Bobo.

"Just about." He closed the Jeep hatch and walked over to them, bummed a cigarette and smoked. Ms. Anglin handed Marie the coffee from her car and Marie gulped it down. They stood in a circle with Bobo and his brothers and the girlfriends.

"You all met Marie?" Ms. Anglin pointed to Marie with an elbow as she took another drink of coffee.

They said no.

Ms. Anglin turned to Ed's girlfriend first. "Marie, this is— I'm sorry, hon, I forgot your name."

"Lynette." She wore black eyeliner and had bleached white-blonde hair that stuck straight out from her head with some kind of perm or something. Her hair had long black roots and she had a tattoo on her neck, a word Marie couldn't read.

"Lynette just moved up here from Georgia," Ms. Anglin said. "And of course you know Ed." Bobo's older-looking brother Ed nodded, and it seemed like he grunted, Marie couldn't tell. He was a little scary-looking up close and in the daylight. Lynette and Ed both wore black T-shirts and jeans like they were on a team of some kind.

"And this is Crystal."

"I've seen you at the parties," Crystal said, "but we've never met, I don't think." She was the heaviest one in the bunch. She wasn't fat, but she was solid, thick around the middle with big thighs in tight blue jeans.

Everyone finished their cigarettes and threw the butts down in the yard. "Let's go!" Bobo said, clapping his hands and rubbing them together. Ms. Anglin opened the back door of his Jeep and caught Marie's eye. She nodded for her to sit in the front seat so Marie got in next to Bobo and they all took off.

THE TOWN OF CRAWFORD was sad even on a Saturday morning. Bobo drove up the hill out of the town, past the cemetery and the gas station, south on the old highway. The farther south they went the wilder it was, Daniel Boone National Forest growing up on either side of the road, broken up here and there by a house or a trailer, canna lilies and Rose of Sharon bushes in the yards.

Ms. Anglin leaned up toward the front seat. "Grandma Etta still not talking to you?" she asked Bobo.

He laughed. "Nah."

"So what's up with that?"

"Who knows, but I got a plan. It's going to take some doing, but we'll be out from under Etta." He tapped his thumbs on the steering wheel.

"So where we putting in today?"

"Thought we'd go down here up above Pennington," he said. "That'd give us a good six-mile piece before the bridge. Good and flat. The water's running okay, for this time of year." He started humming a song, then Ms. Anglin started singing it, some song about wheels and destiny Marie had never heard of. But they seemed to know every word and sang it until they pulled off the road into some tall weeds, beside a trail that led down into some trees, and the river below that.

Marie could see the river, brown and green with sunlight on it. It looked warm and cool at the same time. Ed and Keith pulled in behind Bobo and everyone got out and hauled the canoes down the bank to the river. When that was done, the brothers drove a couple of their cars down river and left them where they would end their trip, down under the interstate bridge.

WHILE THEY WERE gone, the women stood around the river-bank. Crystal started talking. She told Marie and Ms. Anglin about her children, her girls she called them. How they were in high school, how they were into volleyball and softball and basketball and how long their legs were and how they wore their thick hair back in a ponytail when they played. Lynette slumped on a tree stump and smoked, her skinny legs stretched out in front of her. Crystal talked on and on, not stopping until Bobo and Ed and Keith returned.

They heard a car pull in and Nikki came down the bank. She looked at Marie but didn't say anything. She made a point to say hello to everyone except her.

"Bobo, I'm riding with you," Nikki said.

"Well, all right. Jilly, you and Marie take Old Red." He picked up a paddle and walked over to Marie for a lesson. "If you want to go forward, paddle this way." He made the regular paddling motion. "If you want to go backwards, this way." He reversed the motion. Marie watched the muscles in his arms as he moved.

"If you want to go to the left, put it on the right side, and vice versa." He demonstrated again, the paddle on either side of his body like he was in a canoe. "Got it?" Marie said yes.

Bobo and Nikki got in their canoe and Ms. Anglin told Marie to sit in the front of theirs. Ms. Anglin pushed it out a little way into the water and got in herself, and they were off. Marie was nervous for the first ten minutes on the water. She couldn't talk and could only concentrate on putting her paddle in the right place. She watched Nikki and Bobo up ahead, watched to see how far they dipped their paddles into the water, how they moved them from one side of the canoe to the other. She finally relaxed when she realized she wasn't going to turn the canoe over, and even if she did they wouldn't drown or be carried off in a swift current or bashed against rocks under the water.

Sometimes they had to navigate around a branch or a little island. Marie kept forgetting which side to put the paddle on to make the canoe turn the right way, she kept paddling on the left side thinking that would make the canoe go left. She messed up so bad once she steered them right into an island that rose up in the middle of the river. The canoe stopped and she could see everything on the little island, tree roots and weeds and rocks. There was a movement there, so quick she could hardly see. Some little movement among the roots and dirt and weeds, and then something slid into the water without a splash. Or did it? It didn't even have a color. It didn't even have a shape. Marie turned to tell Ms. Anglin, but it was already gone, and she couldn't explain it. How do you describe a movement without a shape or a color?

The water was flat and slow moving, with yellow leaves scattered here and there. Marie looked at the trees and watched the four canoes moving down the river. All that hard color, dark green and dark red of the canoes cut against the light green and brown of the water and the trees all around. The brothers lined their canoes up, three across the river, with Bobo in the middle. Marie and Ms. Anglin followed behind. They were all handsome from behind, especially Bobo. He had his shirt off, sunshine on his back and shoulder muscles.

They moved down the river for a couple hours. Marie thought of them as the first people ever on the river. There wasn't a house or car or even another person anywhere around, just trees and sky and water. There were times when everyone was quiet. Then, before they could see it, they heard the interstate bridge, the whine of cars and big trucks passing over. The bridge stretched across the river, white and shining high above them. They paddled to a muddy place under the bridge where Bobo's Jeep and one of the other cars were parked. They pulled out the canoes and rested for a minute. Nikki waded out into the river, her shorts rolled up high. She had on the kind of sandals that were meant to get wet, rubber bottomed with soles meant to walk on river rocks. Marie wanted a pair.

Ms. Anglin went up into the woods to use the bathroom. She made a big deal out of telling everybody where she was going and what she was doing.

Bobo stood beside Marie and offered her a cigarette. "Well, what'd you think?"

"I liked it."

"All right," he said. "We'll turn you into a river rat yet."

Then they heard Ms. Anglin screaming *Help! Help!* from up in the woods, in a way that was serious and scared.

"Ho shit, that don't sound good," Bobo said.

They followed her yells until they could see her sitting on a rock, cussing and holding her ankle. "Dammit Bobo, I got bit."

Bobo scanned the ground around her, then squatted beside her. "Let me see." She took her hands away from her ankle. Two red holes in the skin right behind the ankle, which looked like it was swelling before their eyes. "Daggone girl." He scanned the ground around them again. "You get a look at it?"

"Not really," Ms. Anglin said. "You think it was a copperhead?"

"No, now it probably wasn't a copperhead," he said. His brothers stood behind him, peering down at the ankle, not saying anything. "But you need to get to the doctor anyway. Come on, let me help you." Ms. Anglin put her arm around Bobo and limped to his Jeep.

"I'll take her on in," Nikki said. "I've got to go to work anyway. Drive us to my car, Bobo." They slammed the Jeep doors and Bobo tore out of there. It happened so fast.

MARIE LOOKED AROUND at who was left and she walked back toward the river. She slipped off her hiking boots and waded into the water. Crystal waded out to her and started telling about a girl in her fourth-grade class who got bit by a rattlesnake. "She said she was picking strawberries. It bit her on the finger. It looked like a bunch of grapes on her finger. A bunch of rotten black grapes." Ed and Keith talked on the bank. Lynette sat near them and threw rocks into the river.

"We all thought she probably got bit at church or something. She didn't die or anything, she was back at school the next week or so." Crystal was still talking.

Lynette threw a rock so close to Marie that water splashed up on Marie's jeans. "Oh sorry!" she yelled.

"Come on out. Feels good," Marie yelled to Lynette, motioned for her to join them in the water.

"No thanks. I'm afraid of drowning."

Marie looked down the river, watched the water moving slow. She saw the graffiti on the base of the bridge, red and blue spray paint, naked women and naked dongs, trash talk about somebody named Ronnie. Ed walked over to Lynette, and Keith went out in the river toward Crystal and Marie.

Later when Bobo came back and they all sat around together, Ed said, "Hope cousin Jill is okay. Hope she ain't dead." He stood behind Lynette who sat in a camp chair. He patted her head right on the black roots of her hair.

"She'll be all right," Bobo said. "Worst case, it was a copperhead and they'll keep her overnight."

Crystal started in again about the snakebite girl from her fourth-grade class. How she was in the hospital for weeks, maybe months. She couldn't remember now but it was a long time. The story kept getting bigger and the snake-bit girl kept getting worse and worse.

Marie went to get a beer. She didn't want to hear about the dead grapes on the girl's finger anymore. When she got to the cooler, somebody behind her said, "Hey." She knew it was Bobo so she didn't jump, she knew he would follow her and she knew he would talk to her out there, away from everyone else.

"Jilly will be all right," he said. "Don't listen to all that. Nikki's a nurse, you know, well, nurse assistant. I've known plenty of people got snake bit. Not a big deal, really, anymore."

Marie nodded and handed him a beer. He moved a little closer to her, and they didn't say anything for a while. "I still don't know anything about you. Except your name."

"That's about all I know about you," she said.

"You know how I got this name, right?"

"No," she lied. She made Ms. Anglin tell her after the first time she met him, but she wanted to hear the story from him.

"Nikki couldn't say Billy. She could just say Bobo when she was little. So here I am, thirty some years later and still Bobo."

"You don't like it?"

"Nah. But what are you going to do? Up in Indiana they call me William. That's worse. WILL-yam. I bet you're named for your grandma or something."

Marie laughed, because he was right.

"That's what I figured. Now that is sweet."

"Thank you," she said.

"So, all I do know is that you're a friend to Jilly Anglin. What else do you do?"

Marie couldn't think of anything about herself that he would be interested in. "This and that. You know."

"Ms. Massey. Doer of this and that."

"Well what do you do, Mr. Owens?"

"Hmm. Well now, what do I do." He got serious. "I got four canoes. I want twelve more. Plus kayaks. Probably just need eight of them. And I need a place, somewhere to set up shop. Right here on the river. I want to call it Owens Outfitters." He looked at her. "So that's what I want to do. That's my plan. Right now it's just talk but I'm going to make it happen."

He took out a couple cigarettes and lit one for her, one for him. "I worked construction up in Indiana, past six months. I did it and I hated it." The way he said the word *hated* made her feel weird, like there was something rotten in her stomach. She wondered if that was what the people who worked for her parents felt about their jobs. "Concrete. But it was a means to an end. You know?"

"Yeah," she said like she knew, but she didn't. She never had an end. There was nothing out there she knew she wanted. Nothing she could figure out in words, anyway.

53

"Well I hated it but I got money for now, probably enough for the canoes and the kayaks. If I can find them for the right price. Then just find us a place down here somewhere."

Marie nodded. He made it sound good.

"Just a little bit more, a little bit longer," he said. Then he looked at Marie, straight in the eye, and was silent, like he was giving her a test. She didn't say anything. She didn't feel like smiling at him so she didn't, she just looked right back at him, not moving her eyes from his, giving him her own test. It didn't scare her. It made her feel real, like she was alive. He bent down and kissed her. He moved in closer, his whole body pressed against her. His mouth was softer than she thought it would be. It moved slow on hers, slow and soft, just kissing, and then he put his tongue in, just a little. Not like high school boys who slobber all over. It was real. When he finally pulled away, he kept his eyes closed.

She kissed him on the cheek while his eyes were closed and kept her mouth there for a minute. She wanted to remember the stubble on his sun-warm skin. She wanted to remember the smell of the muddy air. She wanted to remember everything about the moment, everything about the day. The way the river water felt on her hand. The invisible snakes. Even the pained look on Ms. Anglin's face and her swelling ankle, which Marie secretly enjoyed but didn't understand why.

EIGHT

THEY ALL DROVE back to Bobo's house like a convoy. Everyone except Ms. Anglin and Nikki. They stood in the yard for a
while, then the brothers and their girlfriends left in their cars.
Marie followed Bobo into the house. The front door opened
into the living room. He sat down on the couch and she sat
beside him. He kissed her and then he kissed her again. Then
he went into a small hallway and opened a door. She heard the
shower running. He stuck his head out. "I'm going to clean up.
Sit tight." He shut the door then opened it again. "Don't go
anywhere," he said, and that made her smile.

The living room had brown carpet, an old green couch, and
kidney-shaped end tables that looked like they belonged on a
spaceship from the 1950s. There was air freshener on every flat
place in the room, and underneath the freshener smell, something

old that she couldn't place. There were only a few things on the walls, a calendar with almost naked girls leaning onto cars, and a big picture of the ocean. There was an 8x10 Olan Mills studio picture of a man and a woman and three little boys. The woman, she guessed, was Bobo's mom because they had the same dark eyes. She had long, straight dark hair and was wearing a brown and white Swiss Dot dress with lace around the collar. The man wore a brown button-down shirt. The boys wore cream or brown sweater vests with big collared shirts underneath. Beside that picture was a 5x7 of a little girl wearing a red Christmas dress. She figured that was Nikki, same eyes as Bobo and their mom.

She heard the shower stop then. Bobo opened the bathroom door and went down the hallway, so she sat on his couch and acted like she hadn't been looking at his pictures. He didn't come into the living room though. He closed the door of another room and stayed in there a long time. She got bored and looked around for a magazine or something. She found a little picture album on the end table underneath a newspaper. It had wedding pictures from Bobo's parents. His dad was smallish, handsome. His mom was tall and thin, which you couldn't tell from the 8x10. Nikki not only looked like her but dressed like her too. In one of the pictures their mom was wearing a peach dress with wooden beads and lace on it like the one Nikki wore to one of the parties.

And there were baby pictures of all of them. In the back of the album were older black and white pictures, Bobo's parents as children, sitting on rickety-looking porches, overlooking dirt yards. Fat-cheeked babies put in the middle of big old car hoods, held steady by an arm belonging to a person not in the picture. Brothers lined up in the middle of a yard, tallest to smallest, wearing overalls or striped shirts and jeans. She heard a door open so she snapped the album shut and slid it back under the newspaper.

"You want to clean up?" Bobo came in wearing jeans and no shirt, and rubbing his head with a towel. "Bathroom is just down there. I didn't even use all the hot water. I even put out a clean towel for you."

"Thanks." Marie went into the bathroom and showered quick. She used his shampoo and then the water went cold. She dried off and put the same dirty clothes on. She looked for a hair dryer under the sink and in the drawers but he didn't have one. Under the sink there was a bunch of papers with a rubber band around them. The title on the first page was *Crankenstein's Synth*. She shut the cabinet door, brushed out her hair and went back to the living room where Bobo was on the phone.

"You need anything?" he asked the person on the other end. He was sitting on the arm of the green couch. He didn't look like boys she knew, he had muscles and a six-pack. He was lean, but there was something stronger about him than any high school boy she had seen with a shirt off. "Well, call me when you're ready, I'll come get you." He hung up and looked at Marie. "That was Jilly. She's all right. They'll let her out tomorrow."

Then he came over, hugged her, started kissing her. "Your hair smells good," he said. His lips were so gentle, just like out by the river, but it still surprised her. "You've done this before, right?" She guessed he was asking about what would come next. She nodded. She wasn't sure if the times with Kyle counted, they all happened so fast. He took her hand and led her down the hallway to his bedroom. He turned on some music. He put his arms around her again, moved with her to the music and kissed her on the neck. He unbuttoned her shirt, slowly. He slid her bra straps down, then undid it and it fell to the floor.

He took his jeans off, and she took hers off too. He held her for a minute there, just looking at her. Everything about him made her body feel different, lit up. He kissed her and laid her down on the bed, moved his naked leg between her legs. He rolled over to his side and took off his underwear. "Let's get those off." He pulled down her underwear, then looked at her whole naked body, up and down a couple times.

He got a condom out of the side table and she watched him put it on. He rolled back over to her. He touched her, kissed her nipple, then moved on top of her. His body felt like stone above her, not heavy, just solid. His hair came down around his face and she liked that. She kissed him as he entered her. He was solid and she couldn't believe she was that alive, couldn't believe they were together like this. They moved back and forth for a long time, slow and easy, and then faster. "Put your legs up around me," he whispered. She did, and it felt different, even better. She kissed him again and he moaned, his face wrinkled. She felt him come inside her and he said, "Oh," so low and so quiet she could barely hear. They stayed like that for a while. He looked down at her and touched her cheek, kissed her nipples. Then he rolled off and sat up, took the condom off and threw it away.

Marie was cold, so she brought the bedspread up to her waist and noticed there weren't any sheets on the bed. He laid down beside her and put his leg up over her stomach and his arm around her. They stayed like that for a few minutes. It reminded her of the picture of John Lennon and Yoko Ono that Ms. Anglin had, the one from *Rolling Stone* where they're on the floor and Yoko has clothes on but John is naked and has his leg and his arm over her. Marie liked the way it felt, being there with Bobo, entangled in his bed.

THE NEXT MORNING when Marie woke up Bobo was already out of bed, sitting at the table with Keith. The table was in a dining area in the back part of the living room in front of a sliding glass door. They were talking about an auction.

"It's not on the river," Bobo said.

"I know that. But I'm telling you, we need to think about it cause that river property don't come up often. Most of it is in the National Forest, and you know that'll never come up for sale."

Bobo leaned back in his chair. "But it doesn't make sense."

"All I'm saying is think about it, bud. That's all."

Marie walked toward them and Keith said, "Good morning, ma'am."

"Coffee is on the counter," Bobo said. He pointed to the small kitchen that adjoined the dining area. "Cups are in the cabinet, not much here for breakfast."

She poured some coffee into a brown cup and sat down at the table with them. It was covered with papers and there was a book called *How to Start Your Own Business*.

The phone rang. The hospital was releasing Ms. Anglin and she needed a ride. "Get me out of this HELL-HOLE!" she shouted.

"All right, keep your gown on," Bobo said. "We'll be there in a bit." He hung up the phone and looked at Keith. "You going with me?" Keith nodded and stood up from the table.

"You sit tight," Bobo said to Marie.

NINE

THAT NIGHT, after Bobo let her out around the corner in her subdivision, Marie shut the back door of the darkened house. She had walked through yards and wet grass so she slipped off her shoes on the rug, held them in her hand trying her best to be quiet and not disturb her sleeping parents. Then there was a flash, the light in the kitchen flipped on. The suddenness of the light scared her, but she didn't look up from her shoes.

She thought it would be her mom. But when she finally raised her head, there was a different hand on the light switch.

"Dad?" she said. It came out involuntarily, like a breath. He stood there, his hair a messy halo around his head. He didn't say anything, just let his hand fall from the switch to his side. He wore a gray long-handle top and gray jogging pants. His beard was as off-kilter as his hair, the effect a circle of brown around his whole head, wild and uncertain where to go. Marie let the shoes drop, no reason to try and keep grass and water off the floor now.

"What's going on here?" he finally asked. He didn't sound exhausted. He didn't sound like he was ready to give up.

She didn't say anything, but moved her arms so her backpack would fall down into her hands. She started across the kitchen. He moved so she couldn't get by him in the doorway.

"Where have you been?" he asked, his arms outstretched. He seemed bigger than the shell he'd wasted away to after Shane died.

"I'm going to bed. To my room."

"Nope," he shook his head. "You're not."

Marie started to turn back to the door she came in, but he stopped her. Spun her back around. "I asked you a question."

"What the hell do you care?"

"I asked you a question and I expect an answer."

Marie shook her head. She saw something in her dad's face she hadn't seen in a long time. It scared her, it always scared her because she knew what it meant. It was the same look she had when she was so angry she could break dishes or rip shit apart.

He grabbed her by the arm and started kicking at her ankles and feet.

"Dad!"

"By God." His teeth were clenched. "By God I'm not—" He tried to say more but the words were garbled, his mouth so taut the sound couldn't come out. He kept kicking her and it hurt the way he had hold of her arm. She dropped the backpack and tried to get away, move back from him but he kept after it, just kicking and kicking until she was backed all the way across the kitchen and into a corner by the door. He still kicked, mostly hitting the wall around her legs. She felt the tears then, and she finally screamed at him to stop.

He didn't stop. He hit her on the arm, then hit the wall behind her, his teeth still clenched. "What do you think you are doing, do you think this is all just a fucking game or something? You think you can come and go as you please around here? You think you been promoted? You think you been promoted to the boss around here?" He kept kicking. "I'll be damned if I'm going to let you turn into some goddamned trashy dope-taking whore." He hit the wall again. "Go ahead and put me in the grave. Your brother started it and now you are going to finish. Go ahead. Just go ahead and put the knife in my heart. Go on."

He stepped back from her then and stopped the kicking. He went to the island and opened a drawer, but didn't find what he was looking for. He opened another drawer and cussed as he knocked the kitchen utensils around. The noise hurt Marie's head. Her tears were still coming. She wiped them with her sleeve.

He found what he was looking for, a long knife with a black handle. He walked back to Marie, planted his feet, pointed the tip of the blade over his heart. "Go on. Go on and fucking do it. Quicker than how you are doing it now. Go on."

Marie shook her head. She looked at his eyes, but could not tell what was going on there. "Please. Please," she said.

"Please what? Please what? You're staying out, doing God knows what. You might as well just get it over with, just do it." He held the blade and told her to take the handle but she wouldn't. "Just put me out of my misery."

His voice was so low now it was hard to hear him.

"Please don't," she said, hoping this would end it.

The knife clattered to the floor. "Then stop this bullshit. Just stop it." He turned away from her and his tears started. "I can't take it." He left the kitchen and went to the living room and laid down on the couch. She picked up her shoes and her backpack and went upstairs to her room. She took her clothes off and got into the shower. She stayed there for a long time, then crawled into bed but did not fall asleep.

THE NEXT MORNING she heard her parents through the wall. It was mostly her mom. They were in the bedroom. Her mom was yelling about how tired she was. How she has dealt with this long enough. How he hadn't helped her, where the hell is he all the time anyway? She never knew where he was, even when he was right in there on the couch. He might as well have died when Shane did.

Marie startled when she heard that. Her mom never said Shane's name, ever, not since he died. Her mom must have startled too, because she stopped for a minute and it was completely quiet in their room.

"Look, she's run off God knows how many times to those God-forsaken people. I'm at the end of my rope here. I can't keep doing this."

More silence. Marie heard their dresser drawer open and shut. Heard another one open, the brass handle's tinny clink when it shut again.

"Where could we even send her?" her dad finally said. The way he said it, Marie knew he was done too. His voice was low and defeated. The madness from the night before was gone.

"I don't know what else to do here. Tell me, what else can we do here?" her mom said. She wanted to send Marie to The Ridge or some other place for messed up kids. Where they lock you in, like a prison. Her mom had decided and it would happen. It was just a question of when.

When her parents were finished fighting and deciding that they would send her to The Ridge, Marie reached under her bed for the container, which was pink, the size and shape of a Zippo lighter, decorated with a red rose imprinted on a spider web. The bottom slid down like a matchbox, and the space there could be used for something small. Marie got out two of the Xanax Ms. Anglin gave her. They were in her mouth when her mom walked into her room. Marie slid the fake lighter under her pillow and swallowed.

"I don't like what's been going on around here," her mom said.

Marie was already over it. "Go ahead," Marie said. "I know what you're going to do. Just do it."

Her mom walked out and slammed the bedroom door.

MARIE STAYED in her room all day, didn't go to school. That night, she put a sweatshirt, a pair of jeans, and some underwear in her backpack. She unlocked her bedroom window and pushed. It wouldn't budge. She checked the lock. Pushed again. She could see the porch roof just below.

She threw the backpack down and hit the window frame with her palm, but something sharp made her pull back. It wasn't a big nail, like her dad would have used. It was a small picture nail, angled into the window so it wouldn't open.

She kicked the wall then she kicked the backpack across the room. Forget it, she said to herself. She just went out the front door, walked down the street to Bobo's car, and they left. Her mom might have called after her, she couldn't really remember, and it didn't matter anyway.

PART TWO

TEN

THE DOOR SHOOK with the knock, like a monster was banging on it. Marie pulled her pants on and put her hair up in a ponytail. In the week she had been staying with Bobo, he had left out early every morning with Keith, left her alone at the house until noon. A man was standing at the front door. She recognized him as the lawyer who had come to some of the parties. He was wearing the same white button-down shirt and khaki pants.

"Bobo here? Who the hell are you?"

"No," she said.

"No, you don't know who you are?" He was sweating. He grabbed the door facing and used it to move himself into the house. "Or no, Bobo's not here?"

Marie had to step aside. He wiped the sweat from his temple with his hand. He looked around the room, eyes not staying in any place for long. Neither of them said anything for a minute.

"Love what he's done with the place," he said. He blinked and licked his teeth. "You don't have a name?"

"Marie."

"What planet did you drop in from?" He walked down the hallway, past the bathroom and the bedroom, to the room Bobo used as an office, and she followed him. He turned the knob but it was locked.

"Goddammit." He rattled the door as he cussed. "Where's the key?"

Marie shook her head.

"Do you even talk? *Habla inglés?*"

"You probably shouldn't even be in here," Marie said. She walked away from him and back toward the kitchen.

He tried to follow her. "When did he leave?"

Marie didn't answer.

"Oh, he's got a bright one this time. Goddammit, I told him to stop messing with these young girls. You all don't know shit." He emphasized the word *shit*, made it louder.

He made it to the living room and fell. Marie heard the noise and came from the kitchen. He was down on all fours. She looked at him for a minute before she asked if he was okay. He raised his head but didn't say anything. After a minute he got up and came toward her. His voice was low and dry. "You tell him Bert came to see him. Think you can handle that?" His face was so pale. She didn't respond.

"You might want to write that down, if you can write. Tell him to call me." He stopped at the table. "Better yet, I'll just wait for him myself." He turned and walked slow to the couch and sat down, then stretched his legs out and laid down right there without another word, and fell asleep. Or passed out or something.

Marie tried to act like there wasn't a strange man sleeping on the couch. She poured cereal into a bowl. She sat down at the table and opened Bobo's book on how to start a business. She crunched the cereal loud because Bobo wasn't there and she didn't care if it woke up the asshole on the couch.

He raised his hand up once, she could see it over the back of the couch. It reminded her of being in church as a little kid, stretched out on the pew between her parents and sticking her arm up, waving at people behind her until her mom made her quit. He wasn't waving at her though, his hand just went up and then fell back down. Maybe he wanted something to drink. If she had been at home, she would have offered him something when he came in, but she wasn't home, she was in Crawford.

The phone rang and Marie jumped. She knew before she answered that it was Keith's girlfriend Crystal. Crystal had called her every day since she'd been at Bobo's.

"What are you doing?" She never said hello, or told Marie who she was, she always just asked Marie the same thing.

"Not much." Marie stepped into the kitchen so that the man on the couch couldn't hear her talking. "Crystal," Marie whispered, "there is a man here, that lawyer. He wants to see Bobo. He looks sick. He laid down on the couch and passed out or something. He's really weird."

"What lawyer? Who are you talking about?"

"The one who's been to some of the parties. Said his name was Bert. He's in there on the couch. It's freaking me out."

"Oh Lord," Crystal said. "Just hang on. I'll be there in a minute. What does he want?"

"I don't know. He just came into the house looking for Bobo. Tried to get into Bobo's office. I don't know."

"Okay, I'm coming over."

Marie hung up the phone. She opened the drawer where the knives were. None of them were small enough to stick in her pocket, but she felt better knowing a couple were in there if she needed them. She wanted to call Bobo but didn't know where he was. She should've asked Crystal.

She heard something in the living room so she peeped around the kitchen corner at the man. He groaned, like something was making him sick. She went in to look at him, and by the time she got to the couch, he had puked all over the floor. She stepped back away from the smell.

"Are you okay?" He didn't answer, he just groaned. "Do you need a doctor or something?"

He mumbled something she couldn't understand. She moved closer, asked him again if he was okay and if he needed a doctor. The smell was horrible and the puke was a splash of orange and pink on the brown carpet. The man wiped his mouth and said something else she couldn't understand, his eyes stayed closed.

She went back to the kitchen and picked up the phone, then put it back down because she didn't know who to call, and Crystal was on her way. She put some water in a glass and grabbed a roll of paper towels. She went to the bathroom and got the small trash can. She took all these things to the couch and put the trash can beside him in case he threw up again. She folded a bunch of paper towels and put them over the puke, careful not to touch any of it. She put the glass on the coffee table in front of him.

"There's some water," she told him.

His eyes rolled open, then shut, and he nodded. His lips parted, but no sound came out.

A few minutes later Crystal knocked on the door and Marie let her in. Crystal looked down at the man stretched out on the couch. She made a face when she smelled the puke. "What in the world," she said.

Marie looked through the front door and saw the man's car in Bobo's driveway, an old BMW with paint peeling off the hood.

Crystal stepped toward him. She shook him lightly on the shoulder. "Hey, Mr. Morris." Her voice was loud. His head lolled a little but he didn't open his eyes. "Mr. Morris, what's wrong?" He made some noise from his mouth but it didn't make any sense, except Marie thought she could hear the word *help* in there somewhere. She thought she heard him say, *I need help.* Crystal must've heard the same thing, because she said, "What do you need help with? What do you need?"

He opened his eyes and said, "Bobo." That was all he said. Crystal looked at Marie and raised her eyebrows. They went to the kitchen. Crystal chewed her bottom lip for a minute. She stuck her head around the corner to look into the living room. "I don't know what to do except wait 'til Bobo and Keith get here." She leaned back against the cabinet, looked at the refrigerator. "You got anything to eat here?"

"Pizza from last night," Marie said.

"I'm starved to death. Didn't eat this morning. Those girls' granny got me all tore up."

Marie opened the refrigerator and took out the pizza box. They heard the man groan again and throw up. They looked at each other. "He's still breathing," Crystal said and went on with the story about her ex-mother-in-law.

When Crystal was on her second piece of pizza, Marie went to the living room to see for herself if he was still alive. She watched his chest move up and down. He had pulled his arms up and he was shivering. Marie went to the bedroom and took down a quilt from the shelf in the closet and laid it over him.

In the kitchen she asked Crystal what his deal was. "Bert Morris. He's a mess, a bad mess," Crystal said. She dropped her voice to a whisper. "He got disbarred or whatever you call it, so he couldn't be a lawyer for a while. Nobody knows what for or what it was about." She kept eating the pizza. "You got anything to drink?"

"Just water. So what else?" Marie listened as she put ice into a glass and ran tap water until it was good and cold.

"Bobo's daddy, Carlos, you met Carlos?"

Marie shook her head.

"Well, Carlos hates Bert Morris. Strange of him to just show up here, out of the blue. He was the lawyer for Carlos' brothers Toddy and Larney back when they went to the pen and, well, I guess he's been to court for all of them over the years really. He was all their lawyer. And then when Bobo had his trouble, he was his lawyer too. Maybe that's why he's here now."

Marie wouldn't ask her what she meant by Bobo's trouble, his legal trouble, she didn't want Crystal to know she'd never heard about it.

"You reckon he's pill sick?" Crystal said. "That's what it looks like to me." She looked at her watch. "I've got to go to work. I don't think he's going anywhere." She took her keys out of her pocket. "Listen, if anything weird happens here you can call me at work. I can come over and check on you at my break but that won't be until about six o'clock. Bobo and Keith should be back by then. Where are those two?"

She left out the front door and Marie was glad she was gone. There was something about Crystal, all her loud constant talking, about everything and everyone, that put Marie on edge. Even her whispering was loud. Marie put the pizza box in the garbage. She checked on the man again. He was still breathing.

Bobo came in a few hours later. He looked down at Bert on the couch. The brownish hair that ringed Bert's head was messed up, and he had kicked the quilt down to where it only covered his feet. Bobo asked Marie what was going on. They went to the kitchen and she told him the whole story as he washed his hands. He asked where the pizza was and she told him Crystal had eaten it. He made a cheese sandwich on white bread as Marie finished the story.

Keith came in and looked at Bert for a minute then went into the kitchen too. He washed his hands and made a sandwich the same way his brother had.

"What'd he want?" Keith asked Marie.

"I don't know. He just wanted Bobo. And he tried to get into Bobo's office."

Bobo and Keith looked at each other and Bobo shook his head, just slightly.

"What are you going to do?" Keith asked.

"Don't look like he's going anywhere right now," Bobo said. "Guess I'll just leave him there for the night."

"What's wrong with him?" Marie asked Bobo.

He just shook his head. "Hard times," was all he said. "Why don't you run out and get us some cigarettes?" he asked Marie, and handed her a fifty-dollar bill.

SINCE MARIE had been at Bobo's house, she had figured her way around the town. She walked down Langdon Street, past the pink trailer with dark purple shutters and the house with the Rottweilers chained to trees. She walked on crumbling sidewalks past the columned churches and the big houses on the nice street leading into town, and up into the town itself. She stopped at the office of Bert Morris, Attorney-at-Law, and looked through the plate glass window at the receptionist desk and the white walls behind it. A painting of a wildcat hung over a black leather couch, a glass table in front of the couch with a few magazines scattered around. She walked on past the auto parts store painted blue and yellow, and up the hill toward the graveyard, to the food mart where she bought cigarettes and Coke.

Bert was still on the couch and Bobo was in the shower when she got back to the house. She went to the bedroom, put on the long T-shirt she'd been wearing as a gown and got into bed. Bobo came in and laid on top of the covers beside her. He was still dressed. Marie could tell he was thinking about something so she was quiet and laid still beside him.

"He was my Boy Scout leader when I was a kid," he finally said. "All of ours, really. Me and Keith and Ed. He taught us how to canoe and camp. All that I learned from him. He was like my second dad. I can't just let him dry up and die."

THE NEXT MORNING Marie got up and went into the kitchen. Bobo and Bert were talking in the living room. Bert was sitting up and drinking coffee Bobo had made. He was gray and trembling and he didn't look at her as she passed through. Bobo sat in the chair beside the couch with his legs crossed, so straight that both his feet almost touched the floor side by side. His elbows were out, resting on the arms of the chair, and his fingers were laced together across his stomach. He looked like a movie star being interviewed on TV. They were talking low, but Marie could hear them from the kitchen.

"I need help," Bert said.

"Yep," Bobo said.

"I got nobody. Nobody in the world to help me."

"You come in here and scared everybody to death."

"You know what I need. You know I'm good for it, Bobo. You know me."

"I do, Bert. In a lot of ways you're more of a dad to me than my own old man." There was a long pause. "But I cannot give you any more on credit. That's just a fact of business. You understand that. You have to understand that, Bert."

Marie got a Coke from the refrigerator and opened it.

"Now you let me take you to Corbin," Bobo said. "We'll take you to Corbin and you can stay there for a few days and get straightened out. Okay?"

Marie didn't hear Bert say anything back, but he must've said yes because they both got up. When Bert stepped down the hall to the bathroom, Marie went to Bobo in the living room. He stood with his hands in his pockets.

"I'll be back in a bit. Taking him to rehab. Why don't you go to the store for us while I'm gone. You can take Bert's car." He handed her some keys. "He probably needs gas so get it filled up too." He pulled out some cash, a couple of fifty-dollar bills, and handed them to her. "Be sure to get us some milk. And something for supper tonight."

Marie said she would. He kissed her on the head as Bert came into the living room. "We'll see you," Bobo said. Bert went out without looking at her, and Bobo closed the door behind them.

ELEVEN

Marie started arranging Bobo's shirts in his closet by color. It felt like something that should be done. He didn't have any polos, like Shane. No pink or light blue or lime green. The colors were all gray or dark green or navy. Most of the shirts were three-button cotton Henleys that looked so good on Bobo's chest. She thought of his body as she hung the shirts in the closet, his straight shoulders and his wide, strong chest.

She went outside to smoke. She sat on the landing with her cigarettes beside her. The lighter was in her hand, it flamed up in front of her before she noticed the gold Denali parked on the street across from Bobo's house. Her parents. They looked at her through the car window. Marie went ahead and lit the cigarette. She blew smoke out toward them, knowing it wouldn't reach across the yard, across Langdon Street.

Her mom didn't wait for her dad to get out of the car, she came straight across the street to Bobo's yard. She stopped a few steps away from Marie and planted her feet, her arms folded across the lemon yellow sweater vest she wore over a white button-down shirt. She didn't say anything until Marie's dad stood beside her. He eyed the crack in the stucco of Bobo's house that ran from the window all the way down to the foundation.

"Well, glad to see you're not off dead somewhere. Glad to see you are alive at least." Her mom's voice was high pitched and trembly. Marie didn't say anything. She told herself she wouldn't say a word until her dad said something. Until he said he was sorry. "We've been worried sick. Why haven't you called? Why couldn't you call? God almighty, Marie. Jesus. I mean common decency," her mom said.

Marie looked past them. She stared at the house across the street. The one with all the toys in the yard, the one where RODNEY SUX DIX was written in chalk across the driveway.

"You are a real piece of work. Your dad and I work ourselves to death to give you and—" Her mom stopped because she almost said Shane's name. "To give you everything you could want."

It wasn't hard to keep silent when her mom said stuff like that.

"What do you have to say here, Marie?"

Marie shrugged and kept smoking.

"Who are these people?"

Marie looked down the street. The trees were just starting to turn. Just like they were along the river.

"Get your stuff. We're going home."

Even this didn't cause her to look at her mom or dad. She stubbed the cigarette on the step even though it was only half gone, and stood up to go inside. One of the Rottweilers from the scary house next to Bobo's barked, her parents both turned to look. Music blared from the front window of that house, the confederate flag they used as a curtain moved in the breeze. One dog strained against its chain in the front yard. The other dog sat, not moving, like it knew it wouldn't do any good.

Marie turned to go inside. Her mom grabbed her by the arm, tried to stop her. "Oh no you don't."

Marie decided that if her mom made the noise like she did at Shane's funeral, if she made that horrible sad noise that sounded like she wanted to die too, then Marie would say something to both of them. She put the lighter in her pocket and pulled her mother's fingers away from her arm. She decided if her dad apologized for the knife thing, apologized for hurting her, she'd go with them, but he didn't. Marie opened the screen door.

"If you don't go with us now, you can forget it," her mom said. "Don't expect anything from us ever again. I mean it."

Marie stepped inside.

"Marie—" Her dad tried to speak, but it was too late, and it wasn't enough.

She shut the front door and locked it with the dead bolt. She closed the living room blinds, and waited. She could hear her parents arguing, could see them through a crack in the blinds. After about ten minutes they left the yard. After about twenty minutes they drove off, away from Langdon Street.

MARIE TOOK OFF her clothes and got into the shower. She cried when the hot water hit her chest. She remembered standing on the platform with her mother in the shop that sold formal dresses. "Turn around," the shop owner said. Marie's eyes were closed but she had to open them then, had to see herself standing under fluorescent lights in a three-way mirror looking like she'd been doused with powder blue satin and dusted with feathers.

"I can't wear this," she said as she turned for them, but they didn't hear. Back in the fitting room she threw the dress on the floor with all the other ones they had made her try.

She didn't come out again until they made her. This time she wore the one dress she picked, the one she knew they'd hate. It was dark purple with a black lace overlay. It looked like a Gothic flapper. They didn't ask her to turn around.

"This is the one I want." She turned for them anyway.

The shop owner called the color *aubergine*.

Marie's mom stepped onto the platform behind her and pulled it in at the waist. "It will have to be altered."

"I don't want it to be tight."

"It has to be taken in here." She cinched it at Marie's chest.

"It's not supposed to be tight," Marie said.

"That blue one is so much prettier." Her mom stood behind her, hands on each side making the dress shape to Marie's body. "Are you sure?"

"This is the one I want." Marie closed her eyes again and waited.

"Well. I guess," her mom said. She let go of the dress.

Marie couldn't stop her mother from making her go to the winter dance with a band geek named Kyle. She couldn't stop her from arranging hair and pedicure appointments to get ready for the dance. Marie couldn't stop her mom at all. Marie's only choice in the whole deal was the dress, even if she didn't get to pick where it came from.

A couple days before the dance her mom took her back to the shop to pick up the dress. At the shopping center she put the car in park and took a deep breath. Marie thought by the way she was breathing that something was coming. But her mom checked herself in the rearview, then unlocked the car doors.

The store owner disappeared into the back and came out holding a white dress bag with the store logo printed in gold. She put it on a hook so that it hung beside the cash register. Then she lifted the bottom of the bag. It showed blue, powder blue.

"No, that's not the right one," Marie said. "Mine was black and purple, I mean *aubergine*, over there." She pointed to the dark end of the dress rack. "Remember?"

"Marie, someone else in Caudill bought that same dress," her mom said. "Gennie Lee called and told me, so I told her we'd take the blue one."

Marie's head throbbed as the bag was lifted to reveal the feathers at the top.

"Honey, I knew you wouldn't want to show up in the same dress."

"Liar," Marie said. "You are such a liar."

"Stop acting like a four-year-old," her mom said in a sharp whisper.

"That's not the one I want."

"We don't always get what we want, Marie."

At that, Marie tore through the store and knocked a dress off the rack near the door. Outside she climbed the steps to the upper level of the shopping center, cussing and walking in the snow without thinking of where she was going, until she was behind the building, cigarette in hand.

Marie walked back down to her mom's car and stood in the cold. She would not go to any dance, not in that dress. When her mom finally came out of the store with her hands full of packages and the dress, Marie busted out, "You don't give a shit if I go to this dance. You just think it will look bad if I don't."

"Marie," her mom said as she opened the car door and put the dress and packages in the back seat.

"Tell me that's not true." She moved closer to her mom.

"This is all I know how to do." Her mom shut the door and started crying. Marie closed her eyes. "This is all I know to do," her mom said again.

Marie stepped away then, hands in her coat pockets, determined not to look at her. But when her mom cried Marie couldn't think straight. She shook her head. "Why do you make me do this stuff I hate?"

Her mom smiled, let out a half-laugh, half-cry. "You'll look beautiful, Marie. Like a snow princess."

TWELVE

Bobo had to go to Williams County late Thursday night to do a job for his grandma Etta. "Last damn time I'm ever going to work for her," he said. "The last damn run." They took Bobo's Jeep because Ed's license was suspended. Bobo said he'd be back in time for Crystal and Keith's wedding on Saturday. He left Marie money, in case she needed anything while he was gone, but she didn't need it. She stayed in the house and cleaned and organized. She borrowed Crystal's shampooer for the carpet, and she scrubbed the bathroom and kitchen linoleum.

Bobo came back late Friday night, but was up early the next morning, gone with Keith to an auction down at Pennington. He came back smiling. "We bought the property," he said. Marie hugged his neck. "Bert says we could operate from town, shuttle people down to the put-in. Said he knows the guy who owns the little bit of riverfront that isn't in the forest. Says he could get us an easement, or something." He beamed, and it felt like sunshine on Marie, it felt like she was lit up too. "Owens Outfitters. It's going to happen," he said, and he hugged her tight.

It was time to get ready for the wedding. Bobo took a shower. She could hear him in the bathroom singing. She had never seen him so happy.

Marie put her makeup on, using the mirror over the dresser in the bedroom. Bobo came in with a towel around his waist and grabbed her from behind. He kissed her neck and said, "It's all coming together." He went to the closet and rifled through a duffel bag on the floor. "I got something for you while I was gone," he said.

Marie sat down on the bed.

"Here we go," he said. "Close your eyes."

"Bobo, what is it?"

"Close them now."

Marie closed her eyes. She felt him sit down beside her.

"Okay, open." He put a small square box with a yellow bow into her hand. Inside was a tiny diamond mounted on a thin white gold band. Marie felt dizzy.

"I didn't know your size but the guy said we could take it to any jeweler and they could fix it for you."

"It's beautiful," she said. She kissed him and she slid it onto her left ring finger.

"You don't ever have to ask. All you have to do is look at that ring and you'll know you are loved." She smiled at him and felt her eyes tear up. "Guess we better get ready now," he said.

Marie put her dress on, brushed her hair, and finished up her makeup. Every few seconds she looked at the ring. It was a little loose and slid around on her finger but she liked the way it felt.

When she was ready she went into the living room and stood by the couch. Bobo came out in a shirt and tie and khaki pants. He grabbed her up and hugged her, kissed her neck. "And to think you're mine now," he said.

"WATCH OUT for the dogshit," was the first thing Keith said to them. He was wearing a gray tuxedo with a hot pink bow tie, standing by a wooden wishing well in his soon-to-be mother-in-law's side yard. The massive deck on the small gray house was lined with alternating hot pink and white bows, big streamers from the bows hung down from the railing and moved in the breeze. The deck had a walkway that led to a gazebo, which was covered with more bows and gauzy white bunting. A dog bellowed in a chain link kennel in the back of the yard. It was a mutt and Marie couldn't imagine the breeds that had come together to make it.

"Go on in, they're all in there getting ready," Keith yelled to Marie, motioning to the house. "And remind Crystal the deal starts at four. Tell her she's not supposed to be late to her own wedding."

Marie went in through the living room door. The room had a low ceiling and was dark. All the trim around the windows was painted black, the walls were light gray.

Crystal and her daughters were in a back bedroom, Crystal sitting in her bra and slip, her girls in hot pink satin dresses with glittery flowers along the bottom hem, matching hot pink shoes, their hair all done up with baby's breath and glitter hairspray. Even though they were wearing dresses, the girls still sat and moved like they were in volleyball or softball uniforms. Nikki stood behind Crystal with a curling iron, taking Crystal's dark hair section by section and twisting it around the barrel.

"Well I sure as hell was not going to wear black," Crystal was saying as Marie stepped in.

"I wanted her to wear hot pink like us," one of her girls said.

"Did you see Momma out there?" Crystal asked Marie. "She's supposed to be ironing my dress."

Nikki had rolled until all of Crystal's hair was spiraled, then she pinned it up, topped it off with glitter hairspray.

"Marie you just wait 'til you get married. You'll be just as big a mess as me."

Marie could imagine her own wedding to Bobo now, by the river or maybe even in a canoe, everybody in canoes except Ms. Anglin who said she'd never go out on the river again. Marie didn't mention the ring. Bobo never actually said they were engaged, he just gave her the ring. She twisted it on her finger.

Crystal's mom, short and loud as her daughter, came in holding the white satin dress up high so that it wouldn't drag the floor. "It's ready!"

As they helped Crystal get zipped up, Marie slipped out. She watched the ground so she could step around the dogshit. She walked to where Bobo and his brothers were, still standing around the wishing well. Someone had put fake flowers into the wooden bucket that hung under the little shingled roof.

People were walking across the yard. Women in dresses, men wearing mostly button-up shirts. The dress Ms. Anglin loaned Marie was Asian-looking, silky black with red piping around the neck and red frog closures at the shoulder. It made Marie feel different and pretty. Like the Owenses.

"So why are you doing this again?" Bobo asked his brother.

Keith shook his head and rubbed his chin. "Boys, I don't know. I guess I just like the regular sex. And all that nonstop talking, I guess I must like that too." Everybody laughed.

Ed's girlfriend Lynette came around the group and asked Marie for a cigarette and a light. She wore a tiny black miniskirt and a white T-shirt and the highest heels Marie had ever seen. "Did you go to Williams County with them?" she asked Marie, and Marie said no. Lynette looked off, then back at Marie. Her black fingernails matched her eyeliner and the roots of her hair. "When did Bobo get back?"

"Last night, about midnight."

Lynette frowned. "Motherfucker," she said low, barely loud enough for Marie to hear. "Ed didn't get home until daylight. Told me some bullshit about traffic on the interstate." Lynette turned away from the group, watched a family come through the yard.

Marie turned too. "Maybe he was working on this stuff Bobo is always working on. This river business."

Lynette bit her lip, moved her head slow back and forth. "This is bullshit. He's been with some woman, I know it." Then she walked off. She looked at the cars parked in front of and behind Ed's car like she was thinking about leaving, but in the end she got into the driver's seat of Ed's car and just sat there.

A FEW MINUTES before four everyone moved to the gazebo. There weren't any chairs. Keith made his way to the center where his best man Carlos and a preacher in a suit stood under another hot pink bow. Someone pushed the play button on a CD player, and Crystal's girls came out of the house and down the walkway, then Crystal herself, escorted by her mother. Crystal didn't walk slow, Marie had never seen her walk slow, and her mother moved just as fast. The ceremony didn't last long. The cake was set up on a table under a covered part of the deck and soon everybody was eating cake and drinking punch or beer and the music was going loud. Everybody seemed happy, except Lynette, who stayed in Ed's car through the whole wedding and reception.

Crystal made Marie dance the Electric Slide with her and her daughters as Bobo and the brothers watched. Crystal and Keith danced their first dance as man and wife. Carlos danced with Nikki. Ed scowled in the corner then danced with Ms. Anglin after she pestered him into it. Marie danced with Bobo. There were so many people dancing it seemed like the deck was moving too, the floor was swaying. After a while, Bobo said to Marie, "Let's try some of this we brought back," so they walked down through the yard to the wishing well with Ed and Keith.

"Grandma Etta should be at the wedding," Keith said. "We should've waited until she was better so she could be here." Carlos came up then, and Bobo set him up, lining out the powder from a crushed pill on a piece of Plexiglas laid across the wishing well. Carlos leaned over with the straw, stood back up and smiled. He looked like a young man, young as Bobo and his brothers in the evening light.

People on the deck were whooping it up, shouting out song requests. Some of the pink bows had fallen off and onto the yard below. Crystal came to the railing, leaned over and looked down into the yard. She saw Keith standing there, and she put her hands up to her mouth and yelled, "Romeo! Romeo! Wherefore art thou Romeo?"

Keith smiled and yelled back something about his Juliet having the best ass in Larkin County and the whole crowd erupted.

Crystal smiled and blew a kiss to Keith and went back to dancing. "We're going to Myrtle Beach tonight," Keith said. "Some hotel she's been to down there. I don't know."

"Where she went on her first honeymoon?" Ed asked.

"Lord, I hope not," Keith said, frowning.

Marie felt warm and happy until Nikki came up and ignored her. It seemed like grade school. Marie decided to go up to her and make her talk, make her say something. "Crystal's hair looked pretty," Marie managed. Nikki just looked at her. Marie tried again. "How'd you learn to do hair like that?"

"Just learned," Nikki said, then walked off. Marie was ready to go then, but Bobo had more partying to do, so they stayed.

Before they left, Marie hugged Crystal, who was drunk and who had changed out of her wedding dress into a black and hot pink track suit that made a swishing sound when she walked. Crystal wouldn't let go of Marie for the longest time, and Marie felt herself melt a little bit. Crystal was giving her a hug like her grandma used to give, a hug that covered every bit of her, and lasted so long. When they finally pulled apart, Crystal held Marie's forearms and said, "I think of you as my sister, I really do." Her words slurred together. "I don't have any sisters or brothers and Keith's family, well, they're all my family now and that makes you my sister, okay?"

It was so sweet, and felt so true, and Marie was drunk enough to say the same thing back to Crystal, and really mean it. "Oh, I love you," Crystal said, and hugged her again. Then Keith came up and led Crystal off, saying they needed to get on the road now, their bags were already packed and he was ready to hit the beach. There weren't enough people left to throw rice or birdseed, it was four in the morning.

91

THIRTEEN

B OBO WOKE MARIE before it was even light outside. "Come on," he said, and slapped her on the thigh through the blanket. She looked out the window of his bedroom, at the orange circles of streetlight on Langdon Street. She pulled on her clothes and packed the two of them lunch in the cooler, plus some extra water, a couple Cokes, all the while expecting Bobo to come back in and ask for her help to get the canoe on top of the Jeep.

When she took the cooler outside after filling it with ice from the trays in his freezer, she saw Bert's beat-up BMW parked beside Bobo's Cherokee. She heard Bobo and Bert in the garage. She left the cooler on the landing and went back inside.

She figured she had some extra time, figured the two men were going to talk for a while, so she put on some makeup. Not too much, just some eyeliner and blush. She put her hair in a braid so it would be out of the way, then sat on the couch looking at a book for a while, and almost fell asleep.

Bobo banged the screen door open and said, "What're you waiting on, girl! Come on!"

When Marie got outside, she noticed Bert sitting in Bobo's Jeep, in the front passenger side. She looked at Bobo. "Is he going?" Then she saw that two canoes were lashed to the roof.

"Bert needs this. I told him to come and go with us. He's going to help us out with the store, help us work, give us advice."

Marie nodded. "Do you want me to stay here?"

Bobo looked like he was surprised at the thought. "No, no. Bert's all right. He won't bite." He patted Marie on the shoulder. "Come on. Let's get crackin'."

Marie got in the backseat. Bert didn't acknowledge that she was there. For a while she tried to follow their talk, but it was all about people she didn't know. Finally she folded her sweatshirt for a pillow on top of the cooler, laid her head on it, and closed her eyes. The men kept talking. Marie couldn't even figure a way to get into their conversation. They talked about people doing things she didn't care about, like running for office or getting divorced. She wished she had headphones or a magazine.

When they got to Pennington, Bobo said, "There it is," and he slowed to a stop in the middle of Main Street, which didn't matter, because nobody else was out that early. They looked up at the building Bobo and Keith and Ed had bought at the auction. The building had been a store, a Pepsi sign hung out over the sidewalk with faint black letters still spelling JONES GRO. The windows were covered with yellowed newspapers.

Bobo parked half in the street and half in a parking space. The sidewalk in front of the place was broken up and weeds were growing in the cracks. They went inside. It was dark even with the lights on. There were green metal shelves that used to hold white bread and Vienna sausages, a checkout line with an old cash register. Everything was dusty and it made Marie sneeze.

Bert and Bobo started taking the shelves apart, leaning the long flat metal pieces against the wall near the front door. Marie tried to do this too, but she couldn't lift a shelf herself. Bobo told her to get the broom out of the Jeep and start sweeping, so she did. They worked for hours like this, Marie sweeping dirt into piles and the men talking and joking as they took things apart.

After they got a whole row of the shelves down, they decided that was enough. To Marie it looked like they had made more of a mess. She couldn't really tell where she had swept. But Bert and Bobo were ready to get down to the river, so they turned out the lights and locked the door.

They drove down the old highway for a few miles, then turned onto a lane that went up into some woods. Marie didn't ask where they were going, she just watched. After a while they came around a curve and there was an opening in the trees, a large log house on a little knob up ahead of them. The house had big windows and a wide porch. A stained glass lamp was on in one of the front windows. It was the prettiest house Marie had seen since she had been in Larkin County.

They stopped in the driveway and Bert got out. He opened the garage door and got into a pickup. Bobo turned around and pulled out of the driveway, and Bert followed him in the truck. They got back on the highway and drove for miles before they pulled off and parked Bert's truck, much farther down river than their last canoe trip. Then Bert got back in the Jeep and they drove back upstream.

"It's been years, you know," Bert said when they got out of the Jeep at the put-in. They unfastened the canoes and packed them down to the river. Bobo and Marie got into one of the canoes and Bert sat alone in the other.

The river was a different world. There were fish moving underneath them. There might be a big fish right under them, swimming along and not even knowing they were above it. That thought made Marie smile, the whole world made her smile, especially when she looked down at her hand with the tiny diamond on it, especially when Bobo splashed river water on her.

Bert paddled ahead of them, and they meandered, floating with the current, paddling only to avoid the little islands or fallen trees. The air still smelled like mud and fish.

"How big a van you think we need?" Bobo broke the silence with this question to Bert, but they couldn't hear his answer because he was too far up ahead. Bobo paddled faster so they could catch up. Marie wanted to paddle backwards, slow them down, but she didn't.

THEY FINISHED the trip and pulled the canoes out of the water. Marie tried to be nice to Bert by offering him a bottle of water. He just held up his hand and shook his head no, didn't say thank you. "You look a lot better than you did when you came to the house," Marie said. He nodded. "I guess you're feeling better." He didn't say a word. "Well, nice talking to you," she said.

He and Nikki could both go to hell. Marie walked to the cooler, called him an asshole under her breath. She opened the water she had offered him. "Is it true you got disbarred?"

Bert looked off, toward where Bobo had gone in the woods. Then he moved toward her. "Who told you that?" He was close enough to cast a shadow over Marie.

"I don't know. Just what I heard."

"Listen up. I'm only going to say this to you one time. I don't know what kind of game you are playing here. I don't know what kind of grand adventure you think you are on. I know who you are. I checked you out and I'm watching you. You better watch your step." He licked his teeth the same way he had done at Bobo's house.

Marie took a drink from the water bottle.

"You think you've moved one county away and you're in some other country?" Bert said.

"So you were disbarred," Marie said. Something about him made her want to say shitty things to him.

Bobo came out of the woods then, looking at the two of them. "Beautiful day out here, on the water, in the sunshine." He grabbed the bottle of water from Marie's hand and drank. "Good to be alive." He screwed the lid back on the bottle. "Now Bert, if we park the van here, then they can have this spot to eat their lunch and whatever. If it's a big group, then we can make two trips in the van to pick them up." Bobo went on about Owens Outfitters and how it would all work.

Marie rolled her jeans up over her knees. She wanted to test the new river sandals Bobo had bought for her. She waded out. The water was so cold, and so fast. It massaged her leg muscles. She wanted to get down in the water and let it massage her arms and shoulders too. She gathered her T-shirt in front and twisted it into a knot, then pushed it up to expose her stomach to the sun. She wanted to take her jeans off, and she would have if it had been only Bobo there. She spotted a big rock out in the middle of the water and moved toward it. She had to go slow because the rocks were slippery. The rock was big enough to stretch out on. She looked at Bobo and Bert standing on the shore. Bobo had his back to her, he was pointing up at the road. Bert was staring at her. He wasn't even trying to hide it. She fought the urge to flip him off. She laid back on the rock and adjusted her T-shirt to show as much skin as possible.

BERT DROVE Bobo and Marie back upstream and then left in his truck. Bobo and Marie drove south to a store called John's Discount that sold all kinds of hunting supplies and camping gear. Bobo stood in the aisle, measuring and drawing the store's display shelves in his notebook. He sketched and sketched, walked around over and over. People would try to get around him in the aisle, but he wouldn't even notice. He just kept drawing. A store worker with a name tag came up to him and asked him if he needed help with anything. Bobo smiled and said, "I like your shelves, man."

Marie stood and watched Bobo, then looked around on her own. The Old Town canoes like Bobo had and the kayaks he wanted were expensive. Even the paddles cost a lot. She looked at tents and guns and sleeping bags. The place made her want to go hiking. Buy some wool socks at least.

On the drive back, when they were almost to Pennington, Bobo said, "Hey, let's go swim. Come on, we've been working hard." He rolled the window down, put his hand out into the warm air. He parked at the same put-in, and they raced each other down the bank, stripping clothes as they ran. Marie's shirt caught on a tree branch. They jumped in and leaned back into the shallow water until the water covered their bodies, only their heads popped out. It was almost evening, they could see the sun going down behind the hills, the sky was light purple and the shapes of the trees against it dark, like a Maxfield Parrish painting she had seen in a book at Ms. Anglin's.

Bobo splashed around her but she couldn't take her eyes from the sky and the shadows against it. Then she saw the shirt she'd taken off, hanging on a tree branch, moving. It was so beautiful, the river passing over her, the color of the sky, her shirt moving like a flag, Bobo splashing near her. She wanted to stop time and stay right in that very spot, that very time.

"Why'd you leave your clothes on?"

She looked over at Bobo. He was naked under the water. She had left her bra and panties on.

"Come on, dip in the water and be healed."

She laughed.

"You must be naked to be born again!" He splashed her and she laughed again. "Naked I say!" He circled around her, splashing her, both of them laughing. "Naked! O ye need to be born again!" She unhooked her bra and threw it toward the bank, but it didn't make it. "And your female woman parts as well!" She slipped off her panties and threw them toward the bank, but they didn't make it either, and sank in the water. Some fisherman would hook her undergarments on down the river somewhere. She didn't care.

"Amen!" he yelled when she was naked. She swam near him and kissed him, then swam away. She swam all the way across the river to the other side then back to him. He took her in his arms, and she turned there, like a mermaid. He held her but not too tight. They swam to the bank where they made out, then he ran to his Jeep and got a blanket and brought it down. They didn't care if anyone came up on them, there in the wide open, small rocks poking Marie in the back through the blanket. Their legs were entwined and she had her head on Bobo's chest. It was getting darker. The evening star came up over the hill on the other side of the river. Everything was amazing.

FOURTEEN

Bobo stiffened when he pulled onto Langdon Street. It took a minute for Marie to figure out why, but as the headlights grew closer she saw what he saw, a guy, leaned up against a car in front of Bobo's house. He was thin, he wore a T-shirt and jeans. "Who is that?" Bobo asked.

It wasn't until they parked that Marie could get a good look. "I know him," she said. She jumped out of the car before Bobo could ask who it was. She hadn't seen Kyle or anyone else from school for weeks. She had thought about him, a couple times, just wondered what he was doing. Bobo came up before she could say anything and stood beside her.

"This is Kyle. From school. He's a friend of mine and Ms. Anglin's." Neither of them moved to shake hands. Kyle kept his arms folded. His forearms were so thin and so pale.

"Ms. Anglin is in trouble," he said. "They fired her and they might put her in jail."

"For what?" Bobo asked.

"I'm not sure. That's just what I heard."

Bobo walked off, started unlashing the canoes.

"Man," Marie said. She relaxed and leaned against Kyle's mom's car. She realized then she didn't have a bra on, so she folded her arms too.

"It's all just happened," Kyle said. He took a deep breath. "I think it's about your brother. I heard your parents found some notes from her, in his things. I thought you should hear it from someone you know."

It was dark now and Marie's hair was still wet from the river. She shivered. "You want some water or something to drink? We could go inside."

"No thanks," he said. His eyebrows were drawn together, the way he did when he was thinking. He watched Bobo. "So when are you coming home?"

"Did my parents send you here?"

"No." He shook his head. "What happened?" He looked at her like he expected an answer. "I mean you just left. Nobody has even seen you."

"My parents, we just can't—" She couldn't figure out how to say everything that had happened, what to leave in, what to take out. Kyle looked at her, waiting. "I don't know," she finally said.

"You coming back to school at least?" His face was so much different than Bobo's. He looked like a baby with soft pink cheeks. He had no idea. How could she put books in a locker, eat lunch in a cafeteria, after living in Crawford? He had no idea at all.

"So, you engaged?" He looked at Bobo's ring on her finger. He was the first person who had noticed it.

Another question she didn't know how to answer. "Not really. I mean, we haven't set a date or anything."

"I came down here to tell you about Ms. Anglin, but I wanted to check on you too. Nobody knew where you were, or if you were okay. Are you okay?" He turned to look at her. She couldn't look back at him but she nodded her head yes.

"Look, I know you don't want me as a boyfriend. But I still have you as a friend, right?"

"Yeah," she said.

"And I was worried."

"There's nothing to worry about."

"Well, I guess since everything is great down here, I'll just be on my way." He never could hide it when he was upset.

"Thank you for coming to tell me."

He took the car keys from his pocket and stepped closer to Marie. So close it made her freeze. So close he might have kissed her. Out of the corner of her eye she looked for Bobo.

"Listen," Kyle whispered. "You call me if you need anything. You remember my number, right?"

"Yes." She looked at him and this time she didn't see baby cheeks. All she could see were his eyes. They were big and sad. Always sad even when he was laughing, even when he was trying to be tough.

ON THE DAY of the winter dance sophomore year, Kyle arrived in a tux with a gray paisley bow tie and matching cummerbund. The corsage shook as he slid it over Marie's hand. In the living room her mom sat them down on the piano bench for pictures. Marie's dad walked by the doorway and her mom yelled to him, "Look here at these two." He poked his head around the door frame, nodded and waved.

"You ready to dance?" her mom asked Kyle as she took more pictures of them standing by the fireplace. He nodded yes, grinning but not speaking so he wouldn't mess up the picture. "Smile, Marie." Her mom brought the camera down away from her eye. "Marie." She sounded polite but her eyes weren't. Marie closed her eyes and did not smile.

They got into Kyle's car and she rolled down her window a crack, his cologne so strong it was hard to breathe. She told him to stop by Ms. Anglin's because she wanted to take pictures too.

"You have her for class?" he asked in his creaky voice.

"Journalism."

He turned on the radio.

"She's cool. We hang out," Marie said. "We party sometimes." She told him to turn into a driveway that led to a brick house.

Ms. Anglin opened the door. "That dress ain't so bad," she said to Marie. She took a couple pictures of them in front of the Bob Dylan poster in her living room. "God, I'm glad I don't have to chaperone this one," she told them when she was done.

Marie sat down at the kitchen table with a beer. She offered one to Kyle, but Ms. Anglin interrupted and asked, "Which one of you is driving?" She didn't sit down with Marie like usual, but stood over near the sink. Kyle stood next to the microwave. The red apple clock above her stove ticked. Ms. Anglin talked about the next edition of the school paper. She asked Kyle why he hadn't taken journalism.

"I'm busy with band, you know."

"So you like band?" Ms. Anglin finally sat down at the table, and pulled out a chair. She patted the seat, inviting Kyle to sit down beside her. "Oh I loved band when I was in high school," she said. They talked about what instruments they played, what their band directors were like. She asked him if he was going to play in college. "God, you wouldn't believe the parties I went to in college," she said, leaning toward him, one eyebrow up. "Wild!"

"They can't be any wilder than Crawford," Marie said.

Ms. Anglin turned to Marie, shook her head. "You're not going to college if you don't get those grades up." She smiled at Kyle.

Marie left the half-drunk beer on the table and went to the sun room to get her backpack. At the door Ms. Anglin said, "Tell Principal Ass-Face I said hello. No, just kidding. Don't do that." She squeezed Kyle's shoulder. Marie froze for a second, then went on out the door without saying goodbye.

KYLE DRANK VODKA with Marie in the parking lot of the school. They sat with the heater and the radio going, car windows cracked. They finished half the bottle and she told him about the dress she should have been wearing, the aubergine one.

"But this one has feathers," he said. "Nice." He cocked his head to one side. "I'd go with the feathers, definitely." He took another swig and passed the bottle back to her.

"I freaking hate this dance," she said, which made him laugh so hard he snorted. His bow tie was crooked, but she didn't straighten it. She took another big gulp of the liquor.

"So let me ask you a question," Kyle said. "You and Ms. Anglin, what is that about?"

"I don't know." She took another drink, then handed the bottle back to him. "We're friends. She and my brother, they're friends."

She reached down into the backpack and pulled out the cigarettes. "You want to smoke?"

He nodded. "Yeah, but not in here. Mom's car."

She took the bottle from him and screwed the top back on, slipped it down into the backpack and slid it under the seat. She flipped the sun visor down and re-applied dark lipstick. Kyle watched her. He watched her like she was telling him a secret. She moved it over her lips slower than usual. She smiled at the mirror to make sure it wasn't on her teeth. He accidentally hit the horn and they both jumped.

Kyle followed her around the cafeteria as she searched for the girl in her aubergine dress. They walked under white tree limbs covered with white lights, stepped around quilt batting on the floor that was supposed to be snow. The cafeteria looked like the Nutcracker or something. Kyle's band mates sat at one table and yelled out to him, "Yo Kylemeister!" He flashed a peace sign back at them. They kept walking. He pointed to a girl in purple on the dance floor, but Marie shook her head, yelled at him over the music, "Too shiny. Mine wasn't shiny."

Finally she gave up and they sat with his band friends. She danced with Kyle and the band geeks in a circle on the dance floor. One of them would dance to the center and do his moves, then dance back out and rejoin the circle. They made her dance to the middle too. She did, and then she danced back next to Kyle just as a slow song started. He bowed and put his hand out, and she took it. They danced slow, turning in a circle on the same spot in the dance floor until she had to run to the bathroom.

She missed the commode a couple times and the powder blue of the dress was mottled with orange. Her hair was half up and half down, some of it getting in the way of the puke and catching bits of it on its way to the toilet. A teacher found her there, and when Marie could stand, she escorted her to the green couch in Principal Ashmore's office. Marie held her hand over her eyes, elbow on the armrest. It kept the room from spinning. In a few minutes the principal brought Kyle in by the arm and sat him down on the other end of the couch.

"I'm very disappointed in you two." He looked down at them, then left the office.

"You don't look so good, Feather Girl," Kyle said.

"Ummg," she said, not wanting to make words.

He shook his head. "They're calling our parents."

"Ung."

"My mom is going to be so pissed. We should call Ms. Anglin to come get us," he said. Marie didn't say anything. "You know her number?"

"We are not calling that slut."

Kyle's head bobbed. He scratched his eyebrow. "I thought you all were friends." He sunk back into the couch, his white tuxedo shirt rumpled.

Principal Ashmore opened the door and came in with Kyle's mom. He leaned back against his desk. "We'll deal with the discipline later," he said. "No excuse for this type of behavior." Kyle followed his mother out of the office with his head down, but gave Marie a little wave as he passed.

"Is there anything else you'd like to tell me, Miss Massey?" Principal Ashmore asked Marie.

In her mind she saw Ms. Anglin squeeze Kyle's shoulder. She saw her snort a line of Oxy with her brother.

He asked again, "Anything at all?"

The room was silent until the principal cleared his throat.

Marie finally shook her head. "No," she said. Her parents arrived. Another wave of nausea came over her then, and she doubled over on the couch, stomach meeting her lap.

FIFTEEN

Bobo told Marie one morning it was his grandma Etta's birthday, and that there would be a party for her out at her house on Chestnut Ridge later that day.

"Will everybody be there?"

"Yeah," he said.

Marie made a chocolate cake from a mix. It wouldn't be like her grandma's chocolate cake, homemade with creamy sweet chocolate icing. But it would have to do.

Before the party, she and Bobo went to the store in Pennington and worked a couple hours. He marked off the area in the back where he wanted to put his office and measured out how much lumber he would need.

"So all your cousins are going to be there?"

Bobo looked at her. "Probably. Yeah. Why?"

"Just curious." Marie was sweeping the floor close to where he was measuring. "Some of them I haven't seen for a while."

"Some of them have fell out with Etta," he said.

Marie kept on sweeping. She hadn't seen his cousin Everett since that night in the woods.

Bobo acted like he didn't want to go to Etta's. He was in a bad mood all day. He wound it out on the road to Chestnut Ridge. Marie was pressed against the back of the seat, cake in her lap. The road followed the creek and the bottom, with the ridge rising up on the other side. Out where the houses thinned, they passed a couple sitting on four wheelers down by the creek. They threw up their hands when they saw Bobo's Jeep round the curve, and he honked back at them. They passed the only church out there, abandoned and vine covered, and then passed the END OF STATE MAINTENANCE sign. The road turned a lighter shade of gray on the other side of that sign.

They pulled onto a gravel driveway that bridged the creek, then circled around to the small white house Marie had seen from the road. A silver fuel-oil tank shaped like a pill sat in the side yard next to a satellite dish.

Bobo parked among the pickups and cars already in the front yard. "Put your purse in the glove box," he told Marie, so she did. "I'm not sure who all is going to be here today." He smacked her on the leg and they got out of the car.

It was weird to see Bobo's cousins in the daytime, their hair slicked down and their shirts on, acting sober. Kids flashed by them and beat them to the door of the house and ran in, letting the door slam before Marie and Bobo could get to it.

Bobo and his brothers called Etta by her name, not Granny or Mammaw, or anything like that. But she had the same kind of school pictures hanging on the same kind of paneled walls that Marie's grandma had. Her house was small and warm too. They walked through the living room. Etta sat at a table in her small kitchen, people moving and making food all around her, getting her birthday lunch ready. She had jet-black hair. She was dark and the lines on her face were darker, dark down in the creases. Her eyes were the same deep blue as her T-shirt. Nobody stopped working when Marie came in, but everyone looked at her. They looked at her and then looked back at whatever they were doing. "Howdy," Bobo said, and kissed Etta on the forehead.

"Mmhmm," she said.

Marie went over and stood beside Crystal who was mixing something in a bowl. She was still holding the plate with the chocolate cake she had baked. "Put it over there," Crystal said, pointing to a place on the counter. Bobo left and went outside.

"That one is too much like his momma," Etta said after the door shut behind him. "And Keith's too much like his daddy."

Crystal rolled her eyes but only Marie could see. "Peel those potatoes if you want something to do," Crystal said. She handed Marie a knife and pointed to a sack of potatoes on the floor. "Get a bowl from over there." Marie could feel all eyes on her as she crossed the kitchen to get to the cabinet, all eyes and especially Etta's. She smiled but the old woman didn't smile back.

"I guess I need a bowl," Marie said. She opened the cabinet. There weren't any there.

"Other side," Etta said. "Up there." Marie found a big metal bowl with other bowls nested in it. She had to take all the smaller bowls out and then put them back in the cabinet.

"Whose girl are you?"

For a second Marie didn't realize Etta was talking to her, but no one else answered. "Me?" She turned to the kitchen table.

"Whose girl are you?"

"She's not from here, Mammaw," Crystal said. "She's from over Caudill."

"Well. Who's your daddy?"

"Oh," Marie said. "David Massey. And my mom is Diane."

"Well, don't know them."

Marie put the bowl on the counter beside Crystal and started to peel. Her back was to Etta. She waited for another question but it never came.

"Seventy-five," Etta said. "Now that's old." She laughed, and it turned into a cough.

Carlos came in and planted a kiss on Etta's forehead. "Hello, Mommy." He was smaller than Bobo, but otherwise was just an older version. "Brought you something." He put a yellow box of chocolates on the table in front of her and sat down in a chair beside her. "How you feeling today?"

"Oh, like a seventy-five-year-old woman. Smothering." She coughed again. "Them boys got half the stuff I asked for in Williams County." Marie watched Crystal, who was listening hard to what Etta said.

"Now, Mommy, you don't need to be worrying about all that today. It's your birthday," Carlos said.

"You better get them boys straightened out."

"Yep." He stood up, kissed his mother on the forehead again.

"They don't need to be messing around down there in Pennington." Etta turned as Carlos walked to the door. "I'm telling you, Carlos. I done told them and now I'm telling you."

"All right," he said.

"Ed's the only one of them I can trust to get done what needs to get done," Etta said.

Carlos stopped with his hand on the door. "I'm going to go on out here and see what's going on," he said. He opened the door that went onto the back porch. Etta got up and went down the hallway. The women in the kitchen started to talk.

"What're they doing down at Pennington?" one of the women asked Crystal.

"Something about canoes. Kayaks or something. Trying to put in a store. I don't know much about it."

Marie kept her mouth shut and listened.

"You got those potatoes peeled yet? Bring them over here." A tall woman showed Marie which pot to dump them in. "Put water over them and set them here on the stove. Put some salt in." She looked Marie over good, up close. "You've never been out here before, have you?"

"No," Marie said.

"And which one do you go with?"

"I'm with Bobo."

While they were talking Marie finished her potato work and then slipped out the back door. All the men sat under a big maple tree in the side yard. Carlos sat with his brothers, Bobo's Uncle Toddy, Uncle Larney and Uncle Goldie. The uncles who gave Marie a beer that time at the party. She hadn't seen them since then. They were shorter than Bobo and his brothers. Their bellies were soft and their faces were hard. Their wives worked in the kitchen, but Marie couldn't put any of them together as couples.

Marie got close enough to hear them talking. She didn't understand anything they said. She heard the words, but they must have been talking in code. "Ever now and then a man needs a blow-out," one of them said.

"Toddy, that don't make sense," said another. "Why would a person fall that way when he could've fell the other way?"

Crystal had told her about them, each one had been to the penitentiary. They didn't look mean, just hard. They looked like men who were paying for their parties. The kids ran around where the men were sitting, hid under their white plastic chairs and ran to the creek and through all the cars and trucks parked in the yard.

Nikki pulled in and got out of her Geo Tracker. She was wearing a long flowing skirt and long gold earrings. Keith walked up to her. "Where'd you get them fish bait ear bobs?" She patted him on the shoulder, shook her head. "So what'd you make?"

"I made pop." She handed him two two-liters of orange and grape, the generic kind from the IGA, then patted him on the shoulder again. She got out more two liters, motioned for Marie to come over, then handed them to her. They set the pop down in the yard, then walked across to Etta's shed and brought out two long tables.

Marie tried to set one up. She pounded on the rusty hinge that connected the legs to the table. Nikki got hers in the right position, came over, hit Marie's, and it popped into place.

Nikki went inside and brought out tablecloths to spread over the tables. They set the pop on one end. Women brought dishes from the kitchen and laid them out until there was no space left.

Ms. Anglin pulled up. Marie and Ed and Nikki watched her get out of her car and come over to the table. She had a dish that was made in an upside down, round plastic cake cover.

"If it ain't the long lost cousin," Nikki said. Ms. Anglin's hair was in a bun. She had sunglasses on. "Where's your mom?"

"She's not coming," Ms. Anglin said. "She made this though." She held up the plastic container. There were layers of what looked like crushed-up Oreos, pudding, and Cool Whip. She pulled back the Saran Wrap from the top. "Dirty pudding."

Keith nodded. "Dirty all right. Where's your guitar? You going to play us some ballads today?" Ms. Anglin said no.

"Thank God," Nikki said under her breath. Marie heard it and smiled. "What are you laughing at, Miss Hawkins County? You think I've forgotten about you? I haven't. I remember."

Marie looked at Nikki, who was so pretty she was hard to look at sometimes. "I remember too, Nikki. You saved me and I never will forget it."

"Well you ought to be thankful," Nikki said. "You better be thankful I haven't seen any more of that shit out of you." Nikki turned and walked toward the house.

"What was that all about?" Keith asked. Marie shook her head.

THE FOOD was laid out on the table but nobody was in line or eating. Marie saw a big rock over by the creek. She walked through the yard, watching for snakes. When she got to the big rock some little girls were already behind it. It was like they had hidden themselves for hide and seek but forgot they were hiding and started playing something else. Marie sat by the creek and watched them for a minute, until they ran off. She took off her shoes and put her feet in the water. She wanted to cup her hands and take a drink, it was so cold, but she knew better.

Someone came up from behind and cast a shadow down on her. She turned and shielded her eyes from the sun and squinted up at the figure, but couldn't make him out.

"Bobo?" she said.

The figure moved back and shook his head. "Nope. Not Bobo." He was at a different angle now and she could see him. It was Ed. His face was like Nikki's and Bobo's, but the proportions were different. His eyes were farther apart, and smaller.

"Hey," Marie said, and she turned back toward the creek. She wasn't sure what to say to him. "Good day for a party." She felt something nudge her back. It was his knee.

"I need to talk to you," he said. He kneed her in the back again. She turned her head and looked up.

"Okay."

"You need to back the fuck off. Stop talking to Lynette and telling her a bunch of crap you don't know nothing about."

"I don't know what you—"

"Yeah. You know. You were talking smack to Lynette at the wedding about me having some woman on the side, and if you know what's good for you, you'll keep your mouth shut and mind your own business." His mouth hardly moved when he said this, and his eyes were like steel beams, straight across, gray, not moving, not doing anything. "Watch yourself."

"Hey young'uns." Keith came up and patted his brother on the back. "What's going on?" Ed didn't say anything and neither did Marie. "Am I interrupting?" Marie looked around at the crowd of men in the yard, who had been joined by the women now, ready to get in line and fill up their plates. "Time for grub," Keith said. "Let's eat."

MARIE GOT IN LINE but Bobo was nowhere to be found. She needed to tell him about Ed, how weird he was, she knew he'd understand. He'd know what to say to her, he'd know what to say to Ed too. She tried to catch Lynette's eye, but Lynette looked away, on purpose maybe. Marie got in line behind a family that didn't look like Crawford, didn't even look like the Owenses. The kids, a middle school girl and boy, stood in front of their parents. They watched the other kids, their cousins, dirty and wet and sweaty, threading through the cars parked in the yard. The dad had a goatee and the woman wore her hair long with bangs. When they talked and joked together, they sounded like Michigan. Marie got out of line. She needed Bobo.

He wasn't by the tree so she went into the house. In the living room there was a picture of an angel with pink and white wings looking over two kids on a rickety bridge, a storm all around them. She called out for Bobo. The hall was empty and she opened a bedroom door but he wasn't there. She opened another door to a room that was lined floor to ceiling with dozens of cases of beer on one side, and cases of vodka and bourbon on the other. She shut that door and left the house.

Outside she got back in the line for food. Crystal stood beside her, fussing about making all the food and then having to get in the back of the line to get any. Marie bit her lip then told Crystal the whole thing, about what Ed said. As she was telling it, Marie was getting madder, and she was getting louder.

"Calm down," Crystal whispered.

"What the hell is wrong with him?"

"*Shhh,*" Crystal said. Ed was standing right behind them. Bobo came up then and stood beside his brother. Marie took a deep breath, relieved Bobo was finally nearby. She took her plate and sat beside an old man in a wheelchair by the maple tree. Someone had gotten him a plate and a cup of grape pop. He fumbled in his pocket for a minute, plate balanced on his thin-legged lap, and pulled something out. Marie saw the glint of silver and watched the man cut his ham with a pocketknife.

AFTER PEOPLE finished eating, they all gathered around Etta and someone brought out a sheet cake with blue and white icing. She didn't smile while everyone sang to her. She didn't look at anyone, but stared straight ahead, until it was time for her to lean over and blow out the candles. "All right Mommy," Carlos said, and patted her on the shoulder. The women from the kitchen cut the cake and handed it out.

The kids ran off to play again, and the adults stood around talking to each other. Then Etta cleared her throat and said, "I got something I need to say here." She had to say it twice before people got quiet and listened.

"First off, I want to say that I've got a lot of grandchildren and great-grandchildren here. The good Lord has give me the days to enjoy them and I do."

Marie watched Bobo and his brothers. Their expressions did not change as they watched Etta.

"Now there is something else I need to say here today," Etta said. "I know a few things about running a business. And a farm. It is a one-person deal. Always has been. Even when Marse was around, it was one person, and when he passed on, I took it up. You look at any business, I don't care if it's a funeral home or a nursing home, or whatever, one person has to be the boss. One person has to be in charge of it. Just the way it is. And now that I'm getting on in years, and my health ain't doing me no favors, it's time for me to think about who's going to take over for me."

Keith looked at Bobo. He didn't move his head, he just moved his eyes like a ventriloquist's doll, white eyeballs rolling toward Bobo, then away. Bobo's eyes didn't move, he put his arms across his chest and stood still.

"Somebody needs to take over before I ain't able to take care of things. I'm seventy-five and I'm tired. And I've thought on this for a long time. And I've prayed about it." Crystal rolled her eyes at that. "And what I've decided now, is that my grandson Ed is going to take over here for me."

Marie saw Nikki's head drop at the word *grandson* and she looked away from her brothers. The brothers didn't move. Marie watched, but Bobo's face didn't change after the announcement. Lynette came up and kissed Ed on the cheek.

"I've thought about this long and hard, and that's my decision."
Etta put her hands on the arms of her chair. "So that's it." She
stood up and went into the house.

Ed put his arm around Lynette's waist. He didn't smile, he
looked very serious, like he was now a businessman. Bobo and
Keith walked away, leaving the couple standing together. Marie
went to the table to help take dishes back to the kitchen. She
picked up a bowl but Crystal took it from her hands. "Last time
I make cole slaw for that woman," she whispered. "She doesn't
even like Ed. Shit, who does. She just wants to stir up trouble."

SIXTEEN

CRYSTAL CAME BY, she didn't even call. Just showed up at Bobo's house and told Marie she needed somebody to go with her to deliver tubs of cookie dough her girls had sold to people, a fundraiser for the volleyball team. "What the hell," Marie said. Bobo was gone off to wherever it was he and Keith went all the time. She didn't see him much. He didn't really sleep anymore.

The first stop was Crystal's mom's, the house where Crystal and Keith got married. A few bows still sagged on the deck. Crystal opened her trunk and unfolded a pink piece of paper. She pulled out three yellow and white plastic tubs with white plastic handles, asked Marie to carry two of them.

Up near the house the TV was on so loud Marie could hear it on the porch. Crystal's mom waddled to the screen door and unlocked it, the dog on top of the couch, barking in the window.

They went in and set the tubs on the kitchen table. Her mom opened a tub of cookie dough and inspected it, then put it in the freezer. Crystal got ready to leave, her mom said they better stay and have some coffee or something, but they had more deliveries to make and they left.

"We're going to Carlos' house now," Crystal said when they got to the car.

"He bought cookie dough?" The thought of Bobo's dad making cookies made Marie laugh.

They drove up Chestnut Ridge past Etta's house and turned into Carlos' driveway. "I'm going to let you do this one," Crystal said. "He's got one macadamia nut, one M&M's." She handed Marie two tubs from the trunk of her car.

"Go on," Crystal said, like she would say to one of her girls.

Marie started toward the house, then she turned around, went back and leaned into Crystal's open window. "You got some of this for me, right?" Marie wanted a warm chocolate chip cookie.

"I got some you can have."

Carlos opened the door before Marie could knock on it. "Hello there," he said. "You making some kind of delivery?" Marie nodded. He stepped out onto the porch and shut the door behind him, before Marie could see much inside the house. "Well, I don't really know what I'm going to do with this, but they seemed to think I could use it." He took the tubs from Marie. "Never made cookies before." Close up, Marie could smell liquor, see that his eyes were red.

From the porch Marie could see Etta's house across the road, small and white, like a cottage in the woods by a stream where a kindly grandma would live. The view Bobo would have had when he was a kid. "You know my ex-wife made me build this porch. But I never use it," Carlos said. It was a sturdy porch, wide and long. Brass hooks were screwed into the beam where Bobo's mom probably hung baskets of fuchsia or begonias. "Guess I just don't have much need for it now." He rocked back and forth on his feet. His toes came up off the porch when he was on his heels. Marie looked over his shoulder, through the curtain on the window in the front door, trying to see in.

"Can I get a drink of water?" Marie said.

He looked unsure but finally said, "Yeah, come on in."

Inside the house, there was garbage everywhere. The only furniture Marie could see for the mess was a recliner covered by a sheet, printed with yellow roses. In the kitchen, cans of vegetables were stacked up two to three high on the table. Boxes of crackers, popcorn, Hamburger Helper, covered the countertop. Dirty dishes sat on top of the cans, stacks of them in the sink.

Carlos put the tubs of cookie dough on top of a pile of something, got Marie a glass and filled it with water. She wished she hadn't asked, but drank it anyway and then left.

Back at the car Crystal shook her head but didn't say anything. She pulled out onto the road. She slowed down and they both looked over at Etta's place as they passed. Then she sped up, her little green Toyota chugging along back down Chestnut Ridge.

They saw a trailer down the road from Etta's they hadn't noticed before. Somebody had dozed a spot for it. It looked like it had just been set up, with no underpinning and some rickety stairs up to the front door.

"I'll be damned," Crystal said, and almost stopped again in the road, and then she did stop. She put the car in reverse and backed up to pull into the narrow driveway. "I'll be damned, Keith Owens." She jumped out of the car and slammed the door.

Marie saw Keith's truck then, pulled in around the side of the trailer. She didn't know what was going on but she wasn't going to miss it. She got out of the car and ran up behind Crystal, who was banging on the door, yelling out, "Keith! I seen your car! You better let me in here!"

"What's going on?" Marie asked. She got no response because Crystal was too busy yelling for Keith and banging on the door.

"You better let me in here, you bastard!" Finally they heard shuffling, and muffled voices inside.

"Keith!" Crystal's face was red. The door flew open and Keith stepped out, almost knocked Crystal off the steps. He closed the door behind him. Marie wasn't sure, but she thought she saw Bobo and Ed in the dark of the trailer too.

"Hey baby." Keith was acting cool.

"What in the hell is going on here?"

"We're just up here helping Ed," Keith said. "He can't get the power on in here."

"We? Who's we?"

"Just me and Bobo and Ed."

"What the hell? You're supposed to be at work, Keith."

He breathed in deep.

"Dammit Keith, we need that job," she said.

"Come on now. He needs our help. He's trying to get this place ready to rent."

"This is bullshit. You better not be doing what I think you're doing in there. You hear me?" She walked away.

"Bobo's in there?" Marie asked Keith.

"Yep." He opened the trailer door and went inside.

"Bad feeling about this," Crystal said when Marie got back to the car. "Whatever it is, it's not good."

"What do you mean?" Marie asked.

"You don't even want to know."

SEVENTEEN

Marie WORE her lucky blue tank top to Nikki's birthday party and Bobo's jean jacket. She didn't really want to go, but Bobo did. They drove all the way to some place down on the lake in Wayne County, some place with condos and a guard shack. Bobo told the guard the name of the guy who was throwing the party, some guy Nikki had met in a bar.

The condo buildings all looked the same, wood and stucco painted different shades of light blue, the buildings an island in an asphalt lake of a parking lot. Bobo parked and clapped his hands together and jogged up to one of the buildings, took the metal and concrete stairs in the breezeway two at a time and banged on the door. Marie couldn't keep up with him, and someone almost shut the door in her face. When she pushed the door in, it hit people because the place was so crowded.

All the men were red-faced and older. They wore golf sweaters and big rings and stood around a wooden bar in the corner of the living room. There were girls in mini skirts who looked Marie's age, and boys in bright colors, boys who weren't yet red-faced like the older men, but were on their way. It was like a bunch of dads at the same party with their kids.

The Owens contingent sat on a beige leather couch. Crystal pulled at a Larkin County High School basketball T-shirt, Keith sat next to her spitting into a plastic cup with a paper towel stuffed into it. Nikki was in the kitchen pressing buttons on a blender full of something red.

Marie sat down on the couch between Crystal and Keith. Crystal shared her frozen strawberry daiquiri, which Marie didn't really want since she'd already drunk half of Bobo's pint on the way down. As Keith was talking about their beach honeymoon, a group of women walked into the condo, women that made Marie nervous because they were so beautiful, so put together. Their perfume clouded the whole room. Almost everything stopped when they came in. They went to the kitchen and hugged Nikki and wished her a happy birthday. Marie watched Bobo, who stood beside the entertainment center holding a plastic cup with a faded UK football schedule on the side. He couldn't take his eyes off those women, and after a few minutes he followed them into the kitchen. Marie could hear them joking in the kitchen like they were old friends.

When she couldn't stand it any longer, Marie went in the kitchen herself. As soon as she set foot on the linoleum, the room went silent. "Hey," she said. The women looked at Marie. Nikki had met them at the bar at the marina, the same place she met the old man who was hosting the party.

"You all got some extra of that?" Marie knew it was stupid, the way she said it, and the way she pointed at the blender. They looked at her, silent and blank. Even Bobo. Finally Nikki told her they were out of cups, she'd have to get one from the bar, and she tilted her head toward the living room corner where all the older men stood. Marie didn't move. "In there. In the living room," Nikki said. Marie nodded, finally leaving the kitchen, passed the men at the bar and went to a back bedroom where all the boys her age had congregated.

She was drunk enough to talk to these boys, and they bummed cigarettes from her. They didn't look at her weird like the women did. Maybe they just could hide it better. They talked like they were from Ohio.

Marie found Keith and they went into the other bedroom and he set up a couple lines for her on a black lacquer dresser. "This is some good shit," he said. Marie smiled. He always said that.

When Marie came out of the bedroom, the condo looked different, darker, like someone had turned off some lights. One of the older men danced with Nikki in the living room to a slow song that came from the entertainment center. His gold bracelet made Marie want to vomit. All the kids her age were gone, probably to the houseboat they had been talking about, some big houseboat they had down at the marina.

She sat by herself in the kitchen and smoked. Her muscles felt funny, like they were lit up, and all of a sudden she needed to move. She needed to see Bobo. She combed the condo for him. Crystal and Keith didn't know where he was. Nikki said she didn't know. Marie asked everyone at the party if they had seen Bobo. She knocked on the bathroom doors and opened the doors to two bedrooms. She panicked. Some of those women had gone too, she couldn't remember which ones. An older man offered her a cold beer from the keg and she took it and drank it down quick.

"Have you seen Bobo?" she asked him.

"Who's Bobo?"

"Tall guy, Nikki's brother?"

"Nikki has a brother?"

"Three. She has three brothers. He was the one wearing a navy blue shirt, jeans?"

The man said, "I don't know. Some of them left awhile back to go to another apartment here I think."

Marie bit her lip.

"Are you related to Nikki?"

"No. Bobo is my boyfriend."

"Oh, I see. So you're from Crawford?"

"Nope."

"Must be a wild place," he said.

Nikki walked by and noticed the two of them talking. She got a beer and came over to them. "This young lady is looking for her boyfriend," the older man explained to Nikki. His teeth were yellow.

Nikki nodded at the man, then looked at Marie. "Bobo's gone, honey." Marie couldn't make herself ask where. "You might as well get used to it."

"But—" was all Marie could get out.

"Don't be a sucker," Nikki said, and moved on to talk to someone else. The man looked like he felt sorry for Marie. She thanked him for the beer and ran out the door, then down the concrete and metal steps.

Bobo's Jeep was still in the parking lot. She stood beside it and looked at all the two-story blue buildings, all the windows, all the breezeways between. Nothing she could see looked like a party, no loud music, no crowds of people. The buildings got darker as she stood there. A big orange light clicked on above her, then a pattern of orange lights came on across the parking lot. It was so quiet there, Marie could hear those lights hum above and around her. She took a deep breath and walked toward one of the buildings. She knocked on the first door on the right, then on the left, then back to the second door on the right, second door on the left, then upstairs and on those doors. Hardly anyone was at home. Except an older couple, who opened the door when she knocked. Marie could see their late supper on the table. They wore matching white sweatshirts. They didn't know anything about Bobo or a party, and they looked out in the breezeway like they thought somebody was with Marie, like they were expecting someone to come out and scare them. Marie thanked them for their time.

At the next building someone was at home at every door. One woman asked Marie if she was okay. "Yeah, I'm fine." Marie put her hand to her forehead as she answered and started to cry. "I'm sorry for bothering you," she said. "I just really need to find him." Marie could see kids sprawled on the couch and floor watching a movie. "I'm sorry. I'm sorry for disturbing you and your family." She walked to the next door but the woman kept the door open, came out into the breezeway, kept watching her. Marie finished up the four doors in that building and moved on to the next one.

She didn't find Bobo. She didn't find any of those women either. She kept an eye on the parking lot, watching his car, and also watching the Alfa Romeo Spider she assumed belonged to one of those women, the one Bobo probably left with. After she had gone through four buildings, she sat on some concrete steps and smoked. She didn't see the cop pull in. She got up and started knocking on doors in the next building, this time starting on the second floor and making her way down. The cop walked up to her as she came down the steps, his hands on his belt.

"Good evening," he said.

When she got to the bottom of the stairs, she leaned sideways onto the wall of the building. "Hey," she said to him.

"You looking for somebody?" he asked. "Got a report of somebody banging on doors and yelling, looking for somebody."

Marie looked away, didn't respond.

"You got any ID on you?" Marie held onto the wall for support.

"Let's walk on out here," he said. She followed him down the concrete walkway toward the parking lot. "You need some help here?" He steadied her by holding onto her elbow.

"I'm fine," she said and they stopped at his cruiser.

"What's your name?"

She thought for a second. "Nikki Keith," she said.

"Say again? I didn't get that."

"Nikki Keith," Marie said louder, feeling her mouth move on every syllable.

"You got a phone number, somebody we could call to come and get you?"

"Why do I need someone to come..." she trailed off.

"Miss, it looks like you're intoxicated and we need to call someone, a parent or someone responsible to come and get you and take you home."

Marie thought for a minute, then she gave him her home number, but with one digit off. She smiled but didn't let him see. She had to turn away when he said into the phone, "You don't know anyone named Nikki Keith?" and then, "Sorry to bother you ma'am." Leaning against his car, Marie gave him another wrong number, with the same result.

Then he made another call, this time he didn't ask her for any numbers. Whoever he called sounded like his boss, and it sounded like he was asking the person on the other end what he should do with her.

"Minor," she heard him say. "Obviously intoxicated, slurred speech, dilated pupils, unsteady on feet," he said into the phone, like he was talking about someone who wasn't standing right there beside him.

She thought about running, but all around her were trees and hills, and the condo buildings, that place hadn't been too helpful the first time so she wasn't going back there, and she couldn't remember even where she had started out the night, she couldn't remember which building had the condo with the old men and their bar. It was useless to run.

"All right then. We're going to take a little trip." He opened the back door of the cruiser, and motioned for Marie to get in.

"I haven't done anything wrong."

"Listen, I cannot leave you out here. It's not safe. I'm taking you to the hospital."

"What? I'm not sick." The words came out slow, she couldn't make her mouth move any faster. "I've just lost my boyfriend. That's all." She rolled her head back and forth against her forearm that was along the roof of the deputy's car.

"You don't know where he is?"

"He's here. Somewhere. I think. I don't know."

"Do you have a number for him?"

Marie released a string of curses then. She wasn't sure why, it just felt like it needed to be done.

"All right," the cop said. "Come on." He guided her into the back seat and slammed the door.

Marie kicked the back of his seat. "Why are you arresting me? Why am I under arrest? I haven't done anything wrong!" Then she was silent. She listened to his radio, the voices calling out numbers and codes like a different language. She leaned on the door and window as he drove. Out there it was black dark, no lights, no houses. Just darkness. She kicked the back of the seat. "Where are you taking me!"

She got no response, so she laid down across the seat and closed her eyes. She imagined the backseat was a boat, and she was rocking on the waves of the lake. She didn't know where they were going in the car, she didn't know where they were going on the boat, she was just rocking. The thought of Bobo with one of those women shocked her upright though, and she kicked the back seat and cussed him, cussed the woman, cussed the Owenses and that asshole Nikki.

The cop didn't say anything and it infuriated Marie that he could just sit up there, driving, not saying anything. Just driving in the darkness to their final destination. "Final Destination!" Marie screamed at the top of her lungs. She kicked the back of his seat again. "Final Destination!" she screamed again. She wasn't sure why, but it felt good to scream.

Then they were in another orange-lit parking lot, this one next to a hospital. Marie cussed again. Something about stringing those words together and hurling them at the back of the cop's head felt good, gave her something to do in the situation. She accused the cop of killing her brother, accused him of getting ready to kill her. He was going to take her into that hospital and she wouldn't come back out, not alive. She knew from the way he wouldn't respond that he knew it too. He couldn't deny it.

She nodded off for a second, and before she could run or get her wits, big double doors of the ER opened, and the cop and a nurse were putting her into a wheelchair.

"Where's fucking Bobo!" she yelled, then her head dropped down to her chest. "You better be taking me to him, you bastards!" she yelled again. She saw people standing at a nurse's station, staring at her. Then her head dropped again.

The nurse and the cop stood above her, talking with a woman doctor. Marie couldn't keep her eyes open to see them, but she heard them. They wheeled her into a room with curtains on two sides. Two other nurses came in. One of them told her they wanted to take blood and urine samples, so they could see if something was wrong, see if she needed medical treatment. Marie shook her head violently, her chin rubbing against her chest because she couldn't raise it up. "Nooo!" she wailed.

The nurses lifted her out of the wheelchair, holding her on each side. "Where's Bobo? Where have you taken him!" Marie cussed, screamed and kicked, got loose and ran for the gap between the curtains. "You can't have me!" But she was too slow, why was she so slow, her brain was moving fast but her body couldn't keep up. She was aware of their tricks and what they were trying to pull. They couldn't fool her, even though she couldn't keep her eyes open for very long. They were bigger, they were faster, but they were not smarter, and she could read their minds, and they meant to do her harm.

The nurses held Marie. The woman doctor directed them to "gown her" and ordered blood tests. Marie kicked, but couldn't reach any of them. She tried to twist out of their grip, but they were too strong and too big. "Rodney, you're going to have to excuse us," one of them said.

"I'll be right out here," the deputy said. The curtain moved behind him. Marie could see his brown polyester uniformed legs through the gap. The doctor left the room too. Marie screamed again, and tried to kick the smirking nurses, but they moved much too fast.

"Okay then." The big women started stripping Marie's clothes off, jerking her lucky blue tank top over her head, unfastening her bra, pulling her shoes off and then her jeans and underwear, and Marie couldn't do one thing about it but shiver in the cold hospital air. They put the gown on her and she got some of her fight back, she tried to spit on them and smack them, but somehow they were too quick. They put her on the hospital bed. They strapped her arms down and then her legs. She strained against the straps but could do nothing to loosen them. She beat her head back against the bed. The nurses stood at her bedside. One of the fat ones shook her head. She wore Sylvester and Tweety scrubs. Marie cussed her. Marie yelled for the cop. She yelled for Bobo. She yelled for Shane.

Then another woman with a little blue wire basket-looking thing with a handle came in. She touched Marie's arm, at the inside of her elbow, poked around at it with her gloved finger a couple times. Went around the bed and did that again to Marie's other arm. Marie gathered all the fluid she could in her mouth, then spit with everything she had at the woman, but it didn't go very far, only made it to the edge of the bed.

The woman looked at Marie but didn't say anything, just kept poking at the tender inside of her elbow. Then she pulled some tubing from her wire basket and tied it around Marie's arm. Marie howled. She knew what was next. The cold alcohol swab, then the needle. She cussed and flailed as much as she could in the restraints, which meant she mostly hit her head back against the bed, and she wailed. The blood collected in the tube on her arm and the woman pulled it off and put another tube onto the needle, let it fill up too. She put stickers on the tubes and set them down into little slots in her basket. She put a Band-Aid on Marie's skin at the needle site, untied the tubing. "All done here," she said to the nurses as she took off her latex gloves and threw them in the trash.

The doctor came back in then. "You and your boyfriend are sexually active?" It was more of a statement than a question.

Marie didn't respond.

"Do you use protection?" The doctor had a deep tan and wore a low cut shirt under her white coat. She was a bitch.

"Can I at least get a phone call?" Marie said, making the effort to keep her eyes open.

The doctor shook her head. "The deputy said you had a chance. You gave him wrong numbers." The doctor left through the slit between the curtains.

Marie, alone, looked up at the ceiling because she couldn't do anything else. Did Shane ever open his eyes and see the ceiling of his hospital room? She doubted it. He never moved, not while she was around anyway. She shook her head back and forth to blur the black rectangles that held up the ceiling tiles above her, they blurred like a nightmare in a movie. She screamed. If Bobo was there somewhere, he would hear her and come to her. She screamed again, but no one answered.

When she came to, the doctor stood over her. Marie started to scream but she couldn't make any sound come out. The doctor's hands were in the pockets of her unbuttoned white coat. Her teeth matched the white of her coat.

"Your blood tests are back. I'm sure you know you tested positive for alcohol and benzodiazepine." Marie hated her. If she wasn't restrained she would've slapped her right in the mouth, right on those white teeth. "We also tested for other things. And the upshot is that you're pregnant."

Marie closed her eyes. That could not be possible. She knew that was a lie and this doctor was a liar and this was part of their plan to keep her locked in this hospital until she was dead.

"You're a liar."

"Nope. Sorry. Afraid not," the doctor said. "You're about two months along. And your baby, if it survives all the drugs you've been putting into your body, will likely be born addicted, go through withdrawal, may have brain defects, heart problems, handicaps."

Marie kept her eyes closed. She felt the tears slide off her face, wet her hair, and fill her ears.

"So, now you know." The doctor left Marie alone then, in the hospital room. Her brain buzzed, and she couldn't make it stop. It hummed and buzzed with no thought in particular, just pictures of people, things from her past.

"Mom," Marie said, low and soft. "Mom," she said again, and then dissolved into tears, and then into sleep.

PART THREE

EIGHTEEN

W HEN MARIE WOKE UP, her mom was there, with her in the hospital. She stayed with her parents three days before she ran away again, back to the Owenses, back to Bobo's house.

She sat at Bobo's table looking through the glass door, planning a garden that would fill up his entire back yard. In the winter light, she imagined a grape arbor in the corner. Next to that, a swing. A gazebo in the other corner, with a stone path to the patio. Apple trees. A raised flower bed, stone retaining wall. Lilacs and snowball bushes. A small vegetable garden that Bobo would till for her. Early peas and greens. Carrots. It would be a lot like Grandma Massey's back yard. In her mind she paged through the seed catalogs her grandma used to get.

As it got dark she looked at the window in the house next to Bobo's. The house was dirty. Whoever lived there had hung a blue towel over the window. Marie could tell when the person turned on the light, they must have had a 200-watt bulb.

The thought of that bulb, in that room, gave her a headache. Everything gave her a headache. Smells especially. Some women talked about getting sick to their stomachs, she just got a headache that hardly ever went away. She'd spent three days that week in bed with one, afraid to even take aspirin.

She looked back at the yard. She thought about pink bleeding hearts, the picture in the catalog showing rows of heart-shaped drops. She remembered they needed shade. That would be the first plant she'd order for the garden.

"Everything has a season," Bobo had said to her earlier in the day. He talked like that a lot now. Like a stoner. "Everything, doll baby." Exactly when Marie had become his doll baby she wasn't sure, but she didn't like it.

She went into the bathroom. She needed to dye her hair again. The red was too much. She was going to go over it with black. The box called the color Jet Set.

"You just have to do it," she said to herself in the mirror. She didn't look good, her face puffy and cheeks red, cheeks matching the weird red color of her hair.

Crystal had brought Marie prenatal vitamins and gallons of milk. Marie didn't want the milk and the vitamins made her sick to her stomach. She stopped taking them.

Bobo was gone more than ever now, gone for days at a time either working at the trailer or at the store down in Pennington. They wouldn't let her do much, they hardly let her in the building. It was so moldy and dusty, she'd always sneeze and cough and Keith usually took her home before she even got started.

She'd make Bobo drive her down there when no one else was around, so he could show her what they'd done and what would be happening next. She made a sign for them with a Sharpie on the back of an old poster they found in the store. She wrote: COMING SOON! OWENS OUTFITTERS! She slipped the sign between the newspaper and the glass and put tape all around it.

Before they did any painting or fixed the cracks at the store Bobo hung up a map. It had the river marked in blue, the Daniel Boone National Forest all in green around that, Sheltowee Trace and the Appalachian Trail marked in red. Lake Cumberland below them and to the west.

"See," he'd say, "we're right here in the middle of all this." He ran his fingertips in circles around Pennington, touching all the other points. His hand shook a little. "Get some of that trail traffic to come over here, get some of those cavers." He pointed to the place in the county that was riddled with caves. He tapped Pennington with one finger. "Then we'll be gold."

It made her temperature go up when she heard him talk like that. The we he was talking about, was him and her. His brothers were in on it, but mainly it was him, and so it was her too, she was right there with him. She was the one he was explaining it all to, the one who heard his plans and how things were going to work. She knew about his notebooks, where he kept his expenses and advertising plans, his drawings of shelves and his plans for the store layout.

SHE TOOK THE TOWEL off her head and combed her hair. When she was done she looked in the mirror. "Maybe it will look better when it dries." She could talk out loud because no one was around. She hung up the towel, it had been ruined by all her hair dyeing in the past month, red and black smudges and drips.

There was a knock at the front door. Marie opened the bathroom door and walked toward the living room. When she got to the end of the hall, she could see two cops on the landing through the window in the front door. She took a step back. They couldn't be looking for her, she hadn't done anything. She hadn't even smoked a cigarette since she found out about the baby. Bobo would know what to do here. He probably knew these guys, probably went to school with them. She wouldn't let them in the house, she decided. She'd go to the door, but she would not let them in.

They were sheriff's deputies and they just wanted to give her a paper. A subpoena to testify at something about Ms. Anglin. Grand jury, it said. She took the paper and they left. She put the paper on the table and got some yogurt and Reddi-wip from the refrigerator, and a spoon. She wondered if Kyle had gotten a paper too. She couldn't call him, she'd have to tell him about being pregnant, and that was not something she was ready to do.

She wouldn't go. It wouldn't be loyal to Shane, telling all his secrets out in public like that. What would happen if she refused? Would they put her in jail? She needed to talk to somebody. Maybe a lawyer. She dried her hair and put clean clothes on and walked into town. She walked on the broken sidewalks and past the boarded-up buildings in Crawford. Men stood out in front of the pool hall so she crossed the street.

Nobody sat at the receptionist desk in Bert Morris' office. She opened the door and could hear people talking somewhere in a back room. She sat down and looked at a magazine. The sheriff's paper was in her back pocket but she didn't look at it. Bert's voice was louder than the other voices. She couldn't make out the words exactly.

She put the magazine down and looked out the big picture window onto Main Street. There were other lawyers in town, maybe she would just go and talk to one of them. She wasn't sure why she had come here anyway. Bert was an asshole. She decided to leave and made her way to the door, but Bert and the men he'd been talking to started coming down the hallway, and Bert saw her. No use in leaving if he'd already seen her, so she went back to the couch and watched Bert say goodbye to the men and shake their hands. When the door shut behind them, Bert, with his hands in his pockets, turned to her but didn't say anything. He had the worst manners.

"Look, I don't want to be here. I got some paper and I need to know what it means."

Bert nodded, still not saying anything.

"But if you don't want to help me I can go somewhere else." Marie started to leave.

"Come on back," he said. He motioned down the hallway he'd just come from with the men.

She sat down across the desk from him in a burgundy colored leather chair. Diplomas hung directly behind his head on white painted walls. He leaned back in his executive chair. "Now, what can I do for you?"

Marie pulled the paper from her back pocket, unfolded it, and put it on the desk in front of him. When he finished reading it, he pushed his reading glasses up on top of his head and leaned back in his chair again. "Yeah. So?"

"I can't go."

"Why not? You planning to be somewhere that day?"

"I just can't."

"So don't. Then they'll get a court order holding you in contempt when you don't show." It was quiet. "Jill Anglin made her own bed."

"I'm not worried about Jill Anglin."

"I'm not going to tell you to disobey a subpoena," he said.

143

"I can't go."

"Do what you want. I'm not telling you to ignore a subpoena though." He handed it back across the desk to her, but she wouldn't touch it.

"I'm pregnant."

"I know." Bert stood up and walked toward the office door, using his arm to show her the way out. "I've got a two o'clock. Divorce client that pays," he said, impatient.

Marie finally stood, took the paper off his desk. "You've been real helpful," she said when she was right up next to him, so close she could smell his Old Spice. He grabbed her arm, fingers pressing down into her soft bicep.

"Look here," he said, "you do not belong here. Don't come here looking for comfort." He released her and she started to walk down the hallway. She could feel him watching her, and when she got to the end he said, "I've got some advice for you." Marie turned around. "The best thing for you to do is go on home, back to your parents." Marie started walking again, past the empty desk, and through the office door onto Main Street.

NINETEEN

Nikki came to the house looking for Bobo and waited in the kitchen while Marie washed dishes. "Where'd you get all them prairie dresses?" she asked. "Did that one come with a teddy bear?" After she found out Marie was pregnant, Nikki started talking to her. Not in a nice way, but she was talking to her. Nikki stuck out her bottom lip, said "Aww, did I hurt her feelings?"

Marie breathed out. She felt fat. No jeans fit. T-shirts hurt her skin. The one dress she could wear looked like a tent with little flowers on it.

"Aww, I did. I hurt her feelings. Am I going to make her cry? Am I going to make Little House cry?"

Bobo came in then with a battery for a nail gun in his hands. "Just the person I wanted to see," he said to Nikki. His hat was on backwards and he was wearing sunglasses even though it was cloudy outside. Marie knew he'd been working at the trailer from the way he smelled. "I need you to do something for me."

Nikki sat down at the table and leaned back in the chair. "Who died and made you God of everything?"

"Watch your smart mouth. I need you to go to the hardware store."

Nikki told him to shut up.

"I'm going to say this one more time little sister so listen up." He was leaning over the kitchen table, leaning over Nikki. She rolled her eyes and cocked her head to the side. Bobo slammed the battery down on the table between them. "You're going to get in the CAR, and go to the HARDWARE STORE and get some lye to finish this batch. Then you're going to take it out to the TRAILER. THIS IS WHAT IS GOING TO HAPPEN." When he said that his eyebrows went up above his sunglasses and stayed there. "Because you agreed to go in on this. And so far, you ain't done nothing towards the end product and so I'm telling you what we need done and we need it done now."

"I don't want to be the go-fer. I want to be out there with you all. I want to know how to do this, Bobo. You owe me that." She pushed her chair back from the table. "What about her?" she said, looking at Marie.

"What about her?"

"Make her go." Marie started to say something, but Bobo shoved the battery off the table and both of them jumped when it hit the floor.

"I said you are going. You are going to do this. Take her if you want." Bobo's voice was low but scary.

"I need some money," Nikki said.

"Jesus Christ!" He let out a string of curses as he went back to his office. He unlocked and threw open the door so hard Marie thought it split. She heard him bang around in there, then he slammed the door again. He threw money on the table.

"Come on Mary Ingalls. Let's go get Pa some supplies."

Marie picked the money up. She counted it quick.

Nikki turned the wrong way off Langdon Street, not the way to go to town, not toward the hardware store. She went north.

"Where are you going?"

Nikki wouldn't look at Marie. "Don't worry your pretty little head, Little House." She turned onto the old highway that went to Hawkins County, to Caudill.

"Why are we going to Caudill?" Marie asked, quiet.

"You can't keep going to the same place buying the same stuff all the time. Bobo doesn't realize. He's an asshole and he's stupid."

Marie hoped they wouldn't go to the hardware store her dad used to go to in Caudill, the one he took her to on Saturday mornings on their way to job sites. They drove the rest of the way in silence. They made a turn and drove past Kyle's house. His car was in the driveway.

"Bobo gave me a ring," Marie said. She hadn't told anyone else about the ring, and now she couldn't wear it because her fingers were so fat.

"I can buy myself a ring." Nikki turned off the main road and onto a street that went up a hill behind the main campus. She pulled into a handicapped spot, put her Tracker in park, leaned back in her seat and closed her eyes. In a few seconds a boy came out of a brick dorm and up to Nikki's window, then he ran around and got in the front seat. Marie was pushed up on the console, almost up against Nikki. He smelled like sandalwood incense and Ivory soap. Marie couldn't make herself look at him. She wondered how he and Nikki knew each other.

"Hey," Nikki said.

"Hey," the boy said. "You got it?"

"Yep. You got cash this time?"

"I got cash."

"All right then."

Marie looked straight ahead. Like neither of them were in the car with her. Like she couldn't see them exchange the pills and the money right over top of her. The boy pushed what Nikki gave him down into his front jeans pocket. Nikki put his cash in her ashtray and shut it.

Marie watched the boy take the concrete steps back up to his dorm two by two, hands in his pockets.

Nikki drove the back roads out to an interstate truck stop near Caudill. She pulled in and put the car in park. Marie watched her disappear into the brown painted building. She came out ten minutes later smelling like fried chicken and cigarettes. She put some more bills in the ashtray. "Let's rock and roll. If boss man knew what I was doing he'd be pissed, since it's Etta got me hooked up. Easy money, you know. Fuck him."

Nikki drove to an old farm supply store and handed Marie money from the ashtray for the lye. "Get two bottles. If they ask, you have a drain that's clogged. No, you have two drains that are clogged." Marie took the money and folded it and put it in her wallet so it would look like it had always been there.

"Go on," Nikki said, biting her fingernail.

A buzzer sounded when Marie opened the door. Inside the store she got nervous and walked all around. She felt the different grades of sandpaper. She put her hand down into a bin of screws, moved them around and felt their sharp ends. She handled the dog tie-outs and the FOR SALE signs. She held up red lamp oil to the light coming in from the front window. Then she made her way to the drain cleaners. She saw the lye and picked it up. The man who worked there looked like a Phys Ed teacher with short hair and keys on his belt. He asked her if he could help. He was so clean, and he smiled. He was wearing a polo shirt.

"No, I'm just looking," Marie said. She put the lye back on the shelf. He stayed near her after that. She felt him watching her. After a few minutes she went to where he was. Something made her want to show him that her hands were empty and she wasn't going to buy the stuff or steal it. He spoke to her without looking at her. "That stuff is bad business. Not good." She glanced at him then, she wanted to apologize to him, but she left the store.

Nikki cussed when Marie came out with nothing. Yelled again and screamed and tore out of the parking lot.

"It's not my fault," Marie said. "If you had done this yourself like Bobo asked you to, we wouldn't be here. It's not my fault."

Nikki went into the next place and left Marie in the car. Marie watched the cars pull in and out. Nikki came out, put her sunglasses down over her eyes. She threw her bag in the back seat. "This is bullshit. Give me my money back." Marie got the bills out of her wallet and put them in the ashtray. Nikki started the car. "Let's go see your good friend Jilly Anglin. How about that? You up for that, Little House?"

They drove down the highway not speaking. Nikki made a sharp left turn in front of a slow-moving Ford to get to Ms. Anglin's driveway. "Oops," she said when she saw Marie put her hands on the dashboard to steady herself.

Nikki opened the door without knocking. Ms. Anglin was on the couch, her foot and ankle monitor resting on the coffee table.

"Brought you something," Nikki said.

Ms. Anglin wouldn't look at either of them, kept her eyes on the television. "No thanks. I've got to do my pee test tomorrow."

The Bob Dylan poster was still on the wall. Ms. Anglin had put a sheet over the cushions of the couch, it looked like she slept there now. Her hair was messy and she reached for a pink camouflage cap to put on. For a second Marie wanted to sit beside her teacher, tell her everything would probably be okay. She wanted to remember the good times for a minute, when Shane was there and they were all having fun.

"Oh, come on. You know how to take care of that business," Nikki said.

"And I don't have any money. I've lost my job, you know. Thanks to somebody." She took her eyes off the television then and looked at Marie.

"I could give you a little credit," Nikki said as she sat down beside her on the couch. Nikki put her foot up too, beside Ms. Anglin's on the coffee table. She looked at the ankle monitor.

"You know they've got me charged with manslaughter? And contributing to the delinquency of a minor. Your parents, Massey." Ms. Anglin was staring at Marie.

"I didn't tell them to do it. In case you haven't noticed I don't even live with them any more." Marie refused to sit down then, or touch any of the furniture in the room.

Ms. Anglin looked back at the television. "I didn't make him take anything. I didn't hold him down and shove it up his nose. You all have friends in high places. Commonwealth Attorney. Bert says there's no way they'll get me on manslaughter. They just charged me with it to make them happy. And I've got to go through all this criminal shit before I can even think about getting my job back." She lit a cigarette. "I heard you got subpoenaed." She looked at Marie and blew out smoke. "What are they wanting you to say?"

"I don't know. I have no idea," Marie said.

"You know if you testify for them my lawyers will ask you about all kinds of stuff, I'm just warning you. I think you should know that, before you go in, that they'll bring up stuff on you."

"What do you mean? What are you talking about they'll bring up stuff on me? What stuff?" Marie asked.

"Like problems you had at school, like with Principal Ass-crap. Like going to the doctor back last year with your friend Makinley and selling all those pills at school. Stuff you probably don't want other people to know about."

"Little House!" Nikki piped up. "Little House, I didn't know you had it in you."

Marie clenched her teeth. "I hope you rot in jail. You're too stupid to be a teacher." She went out the door and into the yard, then onto the shoulder of the highway, and started walking.

THERE ARE THINGS on the shoulder of a highway you can't see from a car. Not just gravel and glass. Black rubber pieces from shredded tires. Squashed french fries. Half-empty bottles of orange juice. She knew she couldn't make it far but she wasn't getting back in the car with Nikki. She heard a car pull up behind her on the shoulder, but she wouldn't look back at it. The driver honked. Marie kept walking. "Get in. Come on," Nikki yelled. Marie didn't stop. "Shit." Nikki put the car in park and jumped out, ran to catch Marie. "Come on, get in."

Marie kept going.

"Shit," Nikki said again. "You want me to get Bobo to come out here after you? He'd be pissed and you know it." Nikki was trying to keep up with Marie but her three-inch clogs kept turning on the gravel. "Could you wait up just a second? Marie? Come on." Marie didn't really even hear what she was saying. She wasn't going to get in Nikki's car. That was all she knew.

"Jill Anglin is a dumbass." Nikki ran to keep up with Marie. Her car was way back behind them now. "She's not even related to us. Not really." Marie wouldn't look at Nikki. It didn't matter.

"Hey, I left her three Oxys. On the house. No way she can keep herself away from that tonight. No way. She'll light up every drug test she takes."

Marie stopped, looked at Nikki.

Nikki shrugged. "What?"

Marie started walking again.

"You know what that means, right? You know she'll go to jail with a dirty piss test, right?"

"Why'd you do that?"

"She's too dumb to be a teacher. You're right. Come on," Nikki said. "Let's go."

Marie's feet already hurt and she was cold. Her headache was coming back. She got in the car and Nikki drove to Crawford.

TWENTY

W HEN THE DAYS started to get warmer, the first thing Marie did after she got up was walk to the gas station that had a food mart in it. The place had panty hose and Tylenol. It had the beef jerky that Shane used to eat.

When she got there, the cashiers were talking about someone she went to school with who was in jail. Marie walked to the Slush Puppy machine, got a large cup and put three squirts of lime flavor in it. She tilted the cup away from her so the spray wouldn't splash up. She put the frozen stuff in, put the lid on and a straw in it, and took a long drink before she made her way to the counter to pay.

The cashiers stopped talking when she stood in front of them. She walked out the door and heard one cashier tell the other one, "She lives with one of them Owenses over on Langdon Street."

When she got back to the house, Bobo was back in his office drawing new plans for the store.

"Get in here. I need some help," he said.

Marie breathed deep and walked slow down the hallway. She'd been up all night with heartburn and she just wanted to rest after her walk. Instead she was going to have to stand beside Bobo and watch him work and measure things on paper.

When she got to the office, he said, "I need the ruler, it's in the kitchen." She walked down the hallway to the kitchen and then walked back with it.

Nikki came through the door. "Yoo-hoo, anybody home?"

"Back here," Bobo said.

"Hey buddy," she said to her brother. She wore a long black and red flowing top over tight bell-bottom jeans.

Bobo was letting Nikki go to the trailer now. The two of them talked about their next batch. Marie wanted to ask Nikki where she got the outfit. Bobo finished his drawing, tore it out from the notebook. "You can't be wearing that shirt out there," he said, pointing at Nikki with the ruler.

"I know, I got a tank top on under this. I'm not stupid."

"Well let's go." Bobo turned to Marie. "See you later."

"Wait, do you need any help out there?" She couldn't stand the thought of another day by herself, alone in Bobo's house.

Bobo shook his head. He stepped away from the door and closer to Marie. "Not yet. Later. Just be patient."

Marie watched as they got into Nikki's car and drove away.

WHEN SHE was alone, she thought about things. Home mostly. She thought about the morning of a golf tournament. She was sitting at the breakfast bar eating cereal. Shane finished scrambling an egg and pushed her off his chair, the one by the window. Her dad came in, poured coffee, had his usual pre-tournament talk with Shane, going over points about the course he'd be on, his competition. "I'll see you out there, buddy." He patted Shane on the back. "Eye of the tiger," he said and went out the door.

"You nervous?" Marie asked Shane.

"Nope," he said, and kept eating.

Their mom came in wearing a polo shirt with Hawkins Southern Golf Mom embroidered on the front. She wore it with Bermuda shorts, and an orange and navy and white plaid belt. She looked at Marie's cutoffs and T-shirt. "You wearing that?"

"Yep," Marie said.

Their mom started loading the cooler. She asked Shane if he wanted Gatorade or water? String cheese? Pretzels? "That place doesn't have any food that's worth a crap. Maybe your dad can run out and get you a sandwich." She dumped ice in on top of everything. "You put sunscreen on?"

"Yeah," Shane said.

"Forty?"

"Yeah."

Marie had worked the tournament the day before, selling hot dogs and hamburgers from a Pepsi trailer parked at the eighteenth hole. They were trying to raise money for a spring break trip for the golf team to Florida. Her mom signed her up. Golf parents did the grilling. It was hot and miserable. The grilling dad got drunk and tried to grab Marie. Then he said, "Looks good, performs good," and kind of growled as he passed her a plate of hot dogs. People at golf courses thought they could get away with anything. They got drunk and said stuff they wouldn't otherwise say. They thought they were somewhere else, somewhere it didn't matter what they said or what they did because nobody would ever call them on it. Marie hated golf courses.

Her mom came back into the kitchen. "Ready?" Marie picked up her plate and Shane's plate and took them to the sink. She got her steno notebook and camera since she was supposed to write an article and take pictures for the school paper. "It's going to be a gorgeous day," her mom said. "Can you help me with this?" Her mom picked up one side of the cooler and Marie grabbed the other, and they loaded it into the back of the Denali. Shane had already loaded his clubs and was sitting in the front seat with his earphones on.

It was a weird memory, but she had been having weird memories of her family, of their normal, everyday life. Marie sat on the couch for a few minutes, trying to get her energy up. Her mind was still in Caudill. She opened the side zipper pocket of her purse and took out a picture of Kyle. They were sitting at Ms. Anglin's kitchen table. He wore his Hawkins Southern Band T-shirt, blue with orange writing. She learned later he bought the disposable camera because he knew she was getting ready to break up with him, and that was his last chance to get their picture together. He drove to the drugstore to send it off as soon as the pictures were all taken. Maybe Ms. Anglin told her that, because he wouldn't talk to her after the breakup. The picture just showed up one day in her locker. He had written the date on the back. Under the date, he wrote, "We Used To Be Friends."

MARIE SAT IN Bobo's Jeep for a minute before she turned the key. She drove away from town toward the river. When she got there, she didn't get out of the Jeep, just sat there watching the water flow by. After a few minutes, she pulled back out. She didn't know where she was going, but she found herself heading north on the interstate. She took the Caudill exit. She pulled into a restaurant parking lot. She sat for a minute, trying to decide if she was hungry, then she pulled out again. She was on the main tree-lined road into Caudill, the one with the big old houses, the road where Kyle lived. She slowed down before she got to his house. When she saw his little red Hyundai in the driveway, she pulled in behind it.

Kyle came to the door wearing shiny basketball shorts and no shoes. No shirt either. "Hey," he said. "What's up?" He leaned out and looked in the driveway, then looked at Marie. "Nothing. I was just in town and thought I'd stop by."

He nodded. "You're coming back?"

Marie shook her head. "Just here for the day, I guess."

"Hold on, I'll be back." He let the door shut. Marie sat down on the low wall by the carport. She should leave, she thought, but she didn't have anywhere to go, no one else to talk to.

As she waited, another car pulled into the driveway, a cherry red Lexus. A blonde got out, wearing clothes like Marie hadn't seen in months, a Coach purse on her arm. It was Makinley. "Oh my God, girl, look at you," she said to Marie when she got close enough to recognize her.

"What happened to your hair?" Marie asked.

"You like it? Mom found this new guy in Lexington. He used to be in New York. Expensive as shit. What'd you do to yours?"

"Dyed it."

"You been to see your mom yet?"

"No," Marie said.

"What are you doing now?"

"Still in Crawford."

Kyle came out wearing the same shirt he wore in the picture in Marie's purse.

"Let's go smoke," Makinley said. They walked down the driveway and across the road to the campus, where they believed no one could see them, or anyone who did wouldn't care. They found a bench under a tree. Makinley offered Marie a cigarette.

"No," Marie said.

"Oh, right." Makinley's eyes were squinty like they sometimes got. She lit one for Kyle and handed it to him. Marie saw that they were together, that Kyle and Makinley were now a couple.

"So what are you having?" Makinley asked.

"Girl." People kept asking, and Marie kept acting like she knew.

"Where are you going to have it? Who's your doctor?"

"Somerset, probably," Marie said. "I can't remember his name. Stitson, Stetson, something like that." It seemed like that was the name of a doctor, somewhere.

"Oh, you've got a man doctor? Ugh."

"Yeah, well, Bobo takes me over there, over to Somerset."

"That's your boyfriend, right?"

"Yeah." Marie told Makinley how Bobo bought the building in Pennington and he and his brothers were working on it, how they were going to have a store there and rent kayaks and canoes.

"Oh," Makinley said in the way Marie knew she didn't believe her, or thought it was stupid a person would have a store there.

"I can take you down there sometime." Marie felt the back of her neck get hot.

"Oh yeah. That'd be cool." Makinley was such a liar.

"He rent camping gear?" Kyle asked.

"He wants to, eventually," Marie said, turning to Kyle and away from Makinley.

It was quiet again.

"So how long you all been dating?" Marie asked the two of them, not looking at either of them.

Makinley cleared her throat. "Couple months? Right, Kyle? I mean, you were gone and you broke up with him."

"I'm just asking," Marie said. "Look at me, it's not like I'm, you know—" Marie held her hands out in front of her stomach, exaggerating the size. Kyle laughed, which made Marie laugh. Makinley rolled her eyes. "It's all good," Marie said.

"So have you seen Ms. Anglin?" Makinley asked Marie.

Marie stopped laughing but was still smiling. "Yeah, I've seen her. She's under house arrest or whatever. She has this thing on her ankle. She can't even go across the street to the mailbox."

"Is she going to go to jail?" Kyle asked.

Marie thought about the Oxys Nikki had left for Ms. Anglin. "She might already be in jail."

"I don't think she deserves to go to jail," Makinley said. "I mean, it's not like she forced Shane to do anything. It's not like she held him down." Marie wasn't smiling anymore. She wanted to say something to shut Makinley up. She sounded just like Ms. Anglin. "Your parents are going to be at that thing, what's it called, grand jury, whatever it is. We're going to be there too."

"Yeah. I'm supposed to, but I'm not going," Marie said.

"They told us they can hold you in contempt and put you in jail if you don't show up," Makinley said.

"Fuck 'em. I'm not worried about it." No one said anything for a minute. "Well, I got to go. I'll see you later." It was no use, Marie couldn't think of anything else to say.

"Bye," Kyle said, after her.

"See you," Marie said, throwing up her hand, not looking back.

TWENTY-ONE

Eᴛᴛᴀ sᴛᴀʀᴛᴇᴅ ᴄᴀʟʟɪɴɢ at seven thirty in the morning. Marie didn't answer the first three times. But on the fourth time, when it was almost noon, she did. Bobo wasn't there. He couldn't tell her what to do if he wasn't there. "I've got a crib for you," Etta said. "I'm going to bring it on over. Bobo there? I can't haul it in myself. I don't think you can either."

"He's not here."

"Well, where is he?"

"I don't know."

"Well, I'll be on over in a bit then."

Crystal came by and brought Marie caffeine-free Coke and a plastic tub full of maternity clothes. She sat on the couch and held up wrinkled jeans she pulled out of the tub. "Now this is good stuff, Marie. Some of this I got from the consignment store in Somerset. Good stuff. Look here." She held out the tag on the jeans for Marie to read and handed them to her.

Marie wadded them up and put them back in the tub. She didn't like it one bit, Crystal giving her stuff. She was nice and all, but Marie didn't want to owe her like that.

Crystal shook her head and made Marie get a piece of paper and a pen. She made a list of what Marie would really need for the baby. A car seat, stroller, crib, playpen. Marie tried to pay attention, but Crystal's letters were so big on the paper it was hard to make out the words.

Neither of them heard Etta knock. Crystal saw her standing on the landing in a pale housedress that snapped up the front, standing there with her hands at her sides. Crystal jumped up and opened the door. "Well, hello there," she said, holding the door open.

Etta didn't move. "Help me tote this crib in here," she said. Crystal nodded and they went outside to Etta's Lincoln. A heavy string was tied around the trailer hitch and up around the trunk latch. Crystal struggled to untie the knot, until Etta breathed heavy and pulled a pocket knife from her dress pocket. She sliced the string and the trunk opened. Crystal got her hands on the crib and pulled it out of the trunk herself. Then she got one end and Etta got the other and they took it into the house.

Marie stood looking at the dusty and cobweb-covered baby bed in the living room. She wasn't supposed to like Etta, she made Bobo's life hell to hear him tell it. But Etta had brought something her baby needed, something that was on the list, and Marie hugged Etta before she even really thought about it. Etta was so bony under her clothes, it felt like hugging a bicycle. "Thank you," Marie said into Etta's ear. These things were so unexpected, the crib, and Etta being nice to her.

"Well," Etta said back.

Crystal put her hand on the top rail and shook it a little. "Sturdy," she said.

"It'll need a mattress," Etta said when Marie finally let her go from the hug. "Used to have one but something happened to it. I guess one of them boys took it." She walked to the table and sat down. Light from the sliding glass door streamed in around her dark head.

Crystal poured Etta some of the caffeine-free Coke. "You want something to eat?" She said it real loud, talking right into Etta's ear. Etta didn't even look at her.

Marie saw the flash of a windshield that caught the sun, the light it threw on the wall next to the table, and she knew that meant Bobo was home. In a few seconds, he came into the house with Keith. Bobo looked at Marie like he wasn't happy.

Crystal wouldn't let Keith hug her. She stood right beside him but wouldn't look at him or talk to him. "Well, be that way then," he said and went down the hall to Bobo's office. Nikki pulled in, and then Lynette and Ed. Nikki came in and whispered something to Bobo. He nodded as she talked. Marie tried to get closer to them, to hear what they were saying, but she missed it. Nikki sat down at the table and talked to Etta.

Crystal carried the tub of maternity clothes to the bedroom for Marie. They left the crib out in the space between the table and the living room so that Marie could clean it up later. "Come on home with us, Marie," Crystal said when they were in the bedroom together.

"Maybe some other time," Marie said.

After Crystal left, Etta motioned for Marie to come over and sit beside her. "Your momma plant flowers?" she asked.

Marie shook her head. "No, but my grandma did."

"I got some bulbs for you out in the trunk. Plant them along about the end of the month and they'll come up this summer." She stood up. First the crib and now flowers. Marie wasn't sure what was going on, but Bobo wouldn't like it.

She followed Etta outside. The old woman swayed side to side as she walked.

Then Bobo was behind them. "What's going on out here?"

"I'm giving your girlfriend some flowers," Etta said. She opened the trunk. Her knobby fingers reached in and grabbed the handles of three plastic grocery bags filled with bulbs. She shut the trunk and handed the bags to Marie. "That one's got white, that one yellow, and that one purple." She made her way to the driver's door, hand on the car as she moved alongside it.

"Bye," Bobo said as he walked away from them, back to the house. Etta opened the car door.

"Thank you for the flowers. And the crib." Marie didn't try to hug Etta again. Seemed like nobody hugged Etta.

"You know, them boys, what they're doing is dangerous," she said. The open car door was making the *ding ding ding* noise because she had left her keys in the ignition. "Not good for a young'un to be around all that mess." She pointed to Marie's stomach. Marie nodded, she didn't know what else to do.

"All right then," Etta said, and drove away in her Lincoln.

INSIDE THE HOUSE, Keith turned some music on, put in some mix CD Nikki had made. Nikki opened a bottle of vodka and they mixed it with the Coke Crystal had brought for Marie. It was a party at two in the afternoon.

Ed was leaning over Bobo on the couch, saying, "Well now, if you're going to cry about it, you might as well just crawl up in the baby bed." Bobo looked at him like that was a dare.

"You wouldn't fit in that crib," Nikki joked.

Bobo walked over to the crib, gave it a shake. "Bet I would." Marie could tell by the way he said it, he was going to try. Nikki laughed and that egged him on.

"Ha ha, Bobo, you look just like a baby, put your thumb in your mouth!" Lynette said, nudging Nikki with her elbow.

"Yeah, looks just about right," Bobo said as he swung his foot over the side. It rested on the thin plywood where the mattress would go.

"No," Marie said, but he didn't hear her.

"Oh, look at the baby, ain't it sweet!" Lynette said in baby talk.

He held onto the rails and brought his other leg over and was in the bed.

"Now, Bobo—" Keith started, but didn't finish.

"See, just right," Bobo said. "*Wah, wah!*" He pretended to cry, and he jumped a little, and the bed crashed to the ground under him, the sides of the crib went sideways, and he fell with it, in slow motion almost. Nikki fell down on the floor too, laughing.

"Shit. Crappy thing," Bobo said from inside the mess of wood splinters and slats.

"It was for a baby," Keith said.

Bobo and Nikki got themselves off the floor and went outside with Ed and Lynette to smoke on the back patio. Keith and Marie stood staring at the splintered mess.

"I bet you could glue it back together," Keith said. "See, right here." He pointed to a rail that had split down the middle. He got down on his knees so he could hold it up, show her where to put the glue. Marie started to cry.

"Oh now honey, this is nothing to cry over. He didn't mean it." Keith stood up and patted Marie on the shoulder. They heard Bobo and Nikki laughing outside. Marie could hardly breathe.

"You got any super glue?" he asked.

Marie didn't want to talk, so she just shook her head.

"I've got some at the house, I'll bring it to you next time I come over. We'll fix this thing right up." He patted her again. "It'll be all right."

Marie left the party and went to the bedroom and locked the door. She cleared a spot on the bed. She hadn't known how much she wanted that crib until she got it. She hadn't even got to clean it up. She didn't have anything, really, from Crystal's list. She wanted a crib now, at least. She wanted a place for her baby to sleep.

The tears ran down from the corner of her eyes into her ears. Her eyes were shut so tight she saw the pattern of the lead in the glass of the front door of her house in Caudill. The frosted oval of glass sectioned off by gray lead lines. She got up and changed her clothes, put on her hiking boots and the only long pants that fit. She found the key, down in her backpack.

The party had moved on. They had gone somewhere in the cars but Bobo's Jeep was still there. Marie got in and adjusted the seat. She closed her eyes again before she turned the key.

SHE PARKED in the same spot where Bobo used to drop her off, down the street by the stone entrance to the subdivision. She walked quick on the sidewalk. All she had planned was to get there. She hadn't thought past that point. She passed the two brick-and-stone houses her parents had built for two sisters and their families. They almost matched. "French Provençal," her mom called the style.

She slowed down when her house was in sight. No car in the driveway, a good sign. She felt for the key in her front pocket.

She cut up through the neighbor's yard, passed by the garage window of her house and looked in to make sure neither of their cars was inside. All she saw was the golf cart they must have brought from the club. She made her way to the back of the house. For a second she wondered if something was wrong. Wondered why her parents weren't home on a Saturday afternoon. She put the key in the lock and it turned. She slipped inside and stood on the rug—silent—listening. When she was sure no one was there, she took off her boots, force of habit from coming home late all those nights. She walked on the cold tile of the kitchen. Nothing had changed in the months she had been gone. Even her mom's purse was on the counter. She froze for a second. If they were gone, she wouldn't have left her purse there. She waited until she was sure there was no one in the house before she moved again.

Marie dug through her mom's purse, through the wallet, but it never had cash in it, this time was no different. She knew better than to take the checks. The only other place she thought she could find cash was in the top dresser drawer in her parents' bedroom, where her dad kept his money clip. She was halfway up the stairs when she stopped, she thought she heard a noise. She stood still and listened but it was something coming from a neighbor's yard. She took a deep breath and started up again.

At the top of the stairs, she looked through her brother's open bedroom door. She could see the navy comforter on his bed, the framed picture of the twelfth hole at Augusta National on the wall. Before she realized what she was doing, she was sitting on his bed. She put her hand down to feel the comforter. She thought about resting there, but knew if she did, she wouldn't get back up, that her parents would find her there, spread out and pregnant in her brother's room. She went to his bulletin board and took down the black and white picture they had used in the school paper for a story on a golf tournament. She put it in her back pocket. She took down the picture of her grandma and grandpa Massey sitting on their porch. She put it in her back pocket too.

Before she could take anything else from his room, she heard the garage door open, and a car door slam. Then she heard the kitchen door open and people come inside. She could make out her mom's voice, but not the other voice, except that it was a man. She heard her mom laugh. Marie could not remember the last time she heard her mom laugh. Marie backed up against the wall next to the bedroom door so that if they came upstairs, they would not see her. The man's voice was low and he talked fast. Marie heard them now on the stairs, talking as they walked up, talking about people Marie didn't know. They went into her parents' bedroom and left the door open.

She knew the angle of her parents' bedroom door would make it impossible for them to see her slip by and down the stairs. She stepped quick and quiet down the hallway, and flew down the steps. At the kitchen door she grabbed her boots and opened the door without a sound. She didn't stop to put her boots on, but walked barefoot to the sidewalk and Bobo's Jeep.

WHEN SHE RETURNED to Crawford, Bobo's house was empty. It was a mess, crib still broken on the floor, chairs on their sides, potato chips scattered on the counters, empty liquor bottles. She left it that way. They could clean it up. His office door was open. She pushed the door open the rest of the way. He kept it locked all the time, but it wasn't like he told her not to go in there.

It was a dark room with no window. There was a table and chair, a calendar on the wall. Someone had written "refill" on

168

certain days of the month. Bobo had tacked up a picture of a river from a magazine.

Marie sat down in the chair. There was a flimsy-looking black two-drawer filing cabinet beside the table, one you could get at Walmart or Kmart. The top drawer was open, just a little bit. She pulled the drawer open a little farther and looked in. There were old newspapers folded up, and under the newspapers, bottles of prescription medicine. Nerve pills, muscle relaxers, pain pills. She covered the bottles back up and closed the drawer. She opened the bottom drawer. There were notebooks and papers and underneath all that was a blue bank bag with a zipper on it, bank logo in white. It was the kind of bag Ms. Anglin kept cash in, took to the bank to deposit in the journalism account.

Marie pulled the bag out of the drawer. It wasn't heavy, but it was fat. She unzipped it. There were more bills in that bag than Marie had ever seen. Mostly twenties, but some hundreds too. She shut the bag and took a breath. She could take some and Bobo would never notice. She could buy a new crib and all the other stuff the baby needed. She thought of Bobo coming in and that scared her. She counted out five hundred dollars. It didn't seem to make that much of a dent in the mess of bills, so she counted out five hundred more. She zipped the bag up, then unzipped it, and took out five hundred more. She stuck the bag back in the bottom drawer. "Fuck you, Bobo Owens," she said as she slammed the drawer closed.

Marie left the office door open just like she found it. She took the money into the bedroom and folded it over, put it in the side zipper pocket of her purse. She took the pictures of Shane and her grandparents and put them down in the same pocket. She put the purse over her shoulder and drove to the Kwick Mart and bought an extra large lime-flavored Slush Puppy.

TWENTY-TWO

THE NEXT MORNING Marie decided that having the money in her purse was not a good idea. She tried to figure out the best place to put it when it came to her.

She divided the money up into three Ziploc bags. She put those bags down into an IGA bag. She put one of the bags of bulbs Etta had given her on top of that. She got the other two bags of bulbs and the shovel from the garage. She went into the back yard. The dirt was packed tight. It was hard to get the shovel in very far. She worked slow, cautious of her belly.

Right then, Bobo got back from wherever he had been. He looked at Marie through the sliding glass door. Then he came out into the yard. "What's going on here?" He reached for the shovel. "Here, let me have a go." He dug deeper and wider than she had been able to. "Looks good to me." He grabbed the IGA bag, the one with the money underneath the bulbs.

Marie got hold of it before he could reach down into it. "No, this one has yellow bulbs in it. I want the other ones, the white and purple to go back here." She grabbed up another bag and started putting the bulbs in. "Looks like we're in good shape here," she told him, hoping he would leave her alone.

Bobo watched Marie put the bulbs into the ground. She stood up when she got all the bulbs from one bag planted. He tried to put his arm around her waist, but she pulled away. "What is it?"

She looked at him. "You broke the crib."

"Well what do you want me to do about it now?"

"The baby needs a crib, Bobo." Marie started crying. She wiped her eyes with the top of her forearm.

"That was an old piece of crap." He walked away from her with his hands in his pockets.

Marie turned back to her work. When she heard Bobo's Jeep pull out, she scooped out the bulbs she had planted. She dug the hole to the depth she needed as quick as she could. She put the bag with the money in it into the hole, shoveled dirt over it, and tamped the dirt down with her foot. She replanted the bulbs on top and covered them over. She stood up, clapped the dirt off her hands, and took the shovel back to the garage.

IT WAS DARK when she woke up. The clock radio said two a.m., but Bobo had been messing with it for some reason, something about the red numbers bothered him, so she never was sure what time it was anymore. Her body felt too heavy to get out of bed. And something weird was going on with her stomach, something new. Pain that spread across the bottom part of what Bobo called her bulge. She thought it might go away if she got up and moved around, but the instant she sat up the pain got worse. She stood but sat back down on the bed, leaned over her stomach and held onto it. She breathed deep like the pregnant women on TV, hoping oxygen would somehow make the pain go away. Marie's hands shook. She stood up, walked slow to the kitchen, and got a glass of water. She put her hand on the countertop to steady herself. The back yard was dark through the kitchen window. The house was dark too, she had only flipped on the light above the sink in the kitchen, hoping not to wake Bobo.

She made it to the living room, laid down on the couch. Was the baby coming? She wasn't ready. She didn't have anything ready. The baby couldn't come yet. Nobody was ready for her. Marie pushed her hands against the bottom of her belly. She closed her eyes and pressed hard. Breathed out through her mouth. Then the weird paisley-shaped flashing lights started in her eyes, which meant another headache was coming.

She got up and ran a hot bath, eased herself down into it. She put a wash rag over her eyes. She tried breathing deep again, but she couldn't calm herself enough to get air all the way down into her lungs. Her baby was coming, she was sure now. She doesn't even have a name, Marie thought. My baby is coming and she doesn't even have a name.

Names that were colors flooded her brain. Blue. Purple. Red. Something different. Rose. Iris. Peony. The baby could be a flower. Or she could be a Diane, after Marie's mom. An Opal, after Grandma Massey. The pain came back and made her sit up in the tub, wash rag falling away from her eyes. She cupped her hands and poured warm water over her belly. Her skin looked yellow against the green tub.

She felt another sharp pain, this one made her yell out. She raised herself out of the tub. She got clean clothes from the bedroom and took them back to the bathroom so she wouldn't disturb Bobo. She sat down on the commode because it was too hard to stand up. She stopped to rest after she put on the underwear, stopped again after the bra, which was so hard to fasten now, it left her out of breath. She stopped again after the socks, and finally the dress. She leaned her head over onto the sink. The porcelain was cool on her face. She stayed that way for half an hour, afraid if she moved the pain would start again.

She heard Bobo walk to the kitchen and then back toward the bedroom, stopping at the bathroom door. He opened it without knocking. "What's wrong?"

She didn't answer right away. She didn't raise her head. She could see him from the corner of her eye. "Just don't feel good," she finally said. Her stomach seized with pain again, she rolled her head on the sink, pressed her hands hard against her stomach again. Bobo left the doorway. She heard the squeak of the box springs when he laid back down on the bed.

She ran another bath and thought, how am I going to do this? A little baby would be there, with them, in the house. She undressed as slow as she had dressed, and got back into the tub. She shut the plastic shower curtain, making the bathtub a dark watery cave. She pressed her palms against her eyes. She felt like throwing up, so she opened the curtain and reached for the little trash can beside the commode. She folded the wash rag into a pillow and put it on the side of the tub. She leaned her head over onto it. When she shut her eyes, she saw a pair of pink baby feet. Pink toes and ankles not attached to anything. Just feet. Then someone handed the feet to Marie in a blanket. "There you go." It was supposed to be her baby, but it was only feet.

Marie sat straight up in the bathtub with the next pain. She must have yelled too, because Bobo came back to the bathroom door. She leaned back in the tub and closed her eyes, and after a minute or two, he went back to the bedroom.

She got out of the bathtub and put her clothes back on. She couldn't go to the hospital, she would never go back to the hospital. She couldn't find her shoes. Even if she wanted to go to the hospital she couldn't go without shoes, she told herself. She got the phone and put it on the coffee table, and laid down on the couch. If she had three more pains, she decided, she would call somebody. The first pain was jagged. The next pain was like a straight line, it happened when she got up to pee. It hurt again when she sat back down.

She picked up the phone. Her hands shook. Her parents were the first people she called. She let it ring three times, then pressed the button to hang up.

She dialed Crystal's number. Keith answered with a sleepy voice. He gave the phone to Crystal.

"Crystal, I think I'm having the baby," Marie said.

"You need to go to the emergency—"

"No," Marie interrupted her.

"If you're having the baby, you have to go to the hospital."

"Help me, Crystal. Please. You know I can't go there." Marie started to cry. She sniffed and wiped her nose on her sleeve. The thought of going to the bathroom for a tissue wore her out.

"I'll be over in a few minutes, but now if you really truly are having this baby I am taking you to the hospital." Marie sobbed and sobbed, but quietly so she wouldn't get Bobo stirred up.

CRYSTAL SHOWED UP in her mint-green tracksuit. She sat down on the coffee table next to the couch. Her hair was a mess, mashed down in the back where she had been in bed. She put one hand on Marie's shoulder. "So what's going on?" she asked.

Marie started crying and couldn't talk. In the time it had taken for Crystal to get there, the pains had mostly stopped. Her head was pounding but the sharp pains in her stomach were gone. She was embarrassed to tell Crystal she had come in the middle of the night for nothing.

"Oh honey. Don't even think about it. So no pain now? You haven't been bleeding have you?"

Marie shook her head and wiped her nose with her sleeve again.

"Here. Let me get you some toilet paper, hold on." Crystal went into the bathroom and came back with the whole roll. "Here, doll." Marie thanked her and blew her nose. "So Bobo's slept through all this?"

Marie tried not to cry but couldn't help it. She nodded her head. Crystal put her arms around Marie and hugged her in a tight, smothering hug, and Marie loosened again, just like she had done at the wedding when Crystal hugged her, only this time Marie hugged back just as tight.

"I'm not ready," Marie whispered into Crystal's ear.

"Honey, nobody's ever ready, not really. The ones who think they're ready are too stupid to know they're not."

Marie laughed and felt a bubble of snot come out of her nose. She let go of Crystal and got another piece of toilet paper. "I don't even have a name for her. I don't have anything for her."

"Let me tell you," Crystal said, "when my first one came, we were a mess. I couldn't rest. I was afraid the baby'd stop breathing, and my husband was almost as bad as I was. You have to let yourself learn it. That's all. And I'll help you, and Keith'll help you, and my girls. You're going to be overwhelmed with the help this family will give you." She laughed and Marie laughed too. "Shoot, you'll probably have Keith over here wanting to babysit. You probably won't even be able to get rid of him or me for weeks."

176

Marie looked at her stomach and was quiet for a minute. Bobo came in wearing gray sweatpants. "What the hell is going on here?" He moved Marie's feet and sat down on the couch.

"Everything's all right. False alarm, that's all. Baby thought she was ready and then decided she wasn't, right Marie?"

Bobo looked at Marie to see if that was true. He looked at Marie's stomach, leaned down close to it. "My advice is to stay up in there as long as you can, buddy. The shit gets hard once you're out." He leaned back and laughed, then looked at Crystal. "You bring hot water and towels?"

"I was ready to take her to the hospital, which I guess is more than some people."

"Yeah, well, I'll leave you two ladies be." Bobo stood up and started back to the bedroom.

"I'm taking her with me," Crystal said, "to stay with us a couple days."

Bobo raised his hand, like he was waving to them, and kept on walking. Crystal looked at Marie. "That all right with you?" Marie nodded, and started to get off the couch. She had to rock back and forth to get the momentum to get up.

She packed her pajamas and some clean underwear and another outfit in her backpack. Bobo was sprawled on the bed. He didn't look at her. She went to the bathroom and got her toothbrush and deodorant. Her shoes were on the patio caked with mud from the back yard. She put them in a plastic grocery bag.

"Is it okay if I go barefoot? " she asked Crystal. "I don't want to get all this mud in your car."

"Well, long as you don't mind being barefoot and pregnant, I don't mind." They got in the car. The clock said five a.m.

When they got to Crystal's, she set Marie up on the couch with pillows and a blanket. "When the girls leave for school, you can go back there in Shasta's room. It's quieter in there." She patted the blanket down over her, rubbed Marie's exposed arms. "You need anything?" Marie shook her head. "All right then. Sleep tight." In the darkness Marie heard the swish of Crystal's tracksuit grow softer as she walked down the hallway.

CRYSTAL WOKE MARIE after the girls left for school, got her off the couch and walked her down the hall to a small bedroom. A twin bed was pushed up in the corner. The walls were painted deep purple. There were wooden shelves with sports trophies and team pictures on one wall, and on the wall above the bed a movie poster. "This room's cleaner than her sister's. If we put you in there, we might not ever find you again."

Crystal shut the door and Marie collapsed onto the bed. The room smelled like hairspray and raspberry body lotion. There was a mirror on the back of the door and all Shasta's ponytail holders and headbands were arranged on hooks. There was a bookshelf with T-shirts instead of books, and a small TV on top. Marie held her eyes open for as long as she could, looking at Shasta's room and all her stuff, everything put in its right place and in order. It was easy to fall asleep in there.

Marie woke up when the door to the bedroom opened. Shasta stood in the doorway. She dropped a duffel bag just inside the room and walked toward the kitchen. "Mom!"

"*Shhh*," Crystal said. Their voices got low. Marie put her feet down. She could keep sleeping, but she went to the bathroom.

Crystal met Marie in the hallway. "Feel better?"

"I should call Bobo to come get me."

"Oh no you're not. You're staying right here, until tomorrow at least. I made chicken casserole. It's going to be fun. We might get wild and watch a movie, paint our toenails or something."

She followed Crystal to the kitchen. Marie felt weird sleeping in Crystal's house when she had a place with Bobo.

"Now sit down," Crystal said. "I'm going to get you some of the best stuff you ever put in your mouth." She yelled to her girls to come and eat. She grabbed a couple dish towels and took a glass dish full of brown stuff from the oven. It smelled like stuffing from the store. Shasta stayed in her room. Crystal, Marie, and Tawn, the younger one, sat around the kitchen table and ate the casserole. They drank Mountain Dew, except Marie, who drank the water Crystal gave her.

"You're sitting in Keith's seat," Tawn said. Her face was like a round pink balloon. "How old are you?"

"I'm seventeen," Marie said.

"I'm thirteen," Tawn said. "Do you go to school?"

Marie shook her head. "Nope."

Tawn took a bite of her dinner roll. She looked at her mom, then she looked at Marie. "Why not?"

"Tawn, let her eat in peace," Crystal said.

"Well, I had to quit. But I'm going back. Sometime."

"She never stops asking questions. You don't have to answer," Crystal said, and she gave Tawn a look.

"It doesn't bother me," Marie said.

Tawn was quiet, but started again. "Do you miss school?"

Now Marie was tired of the questions. She wished Crystal would tell her to hush.

"No. Well, yeah. Sometimes I miss my friends."

WHEN THEY LEFT, Marie washed the dishes and wiped off the counters and the kitchen table. She put the Mountain Dew in the refrigerator. She had to move things around in there, leftovers and lunchmeat and jars of homemade jelly, to make room for it.

With the house empty, Marie looked at the family pictures in the living room and on both sides of the hallway. Lots of them were in frames that had the word *family* on them. There was a picture of the girls in pastel dresses standing in the back yard. Pictures of them as babies, toddlers, and school pictures with front teeth missing.

She sat down on Crystal's hunter green and burgundy plaid couch. She noticed that even the blanket she had slept under the night before had a picture of the girls on it, and the message *Happy Birthday Momma!* in burgundy script at the bottom. There weren't any blankets with pictures on them at her house in Caudill. Her mom would have put them in the upstairs hall closet.

Later that night, Crystal came out of the bathroom with nail polish. She propped Marie's feet on a pillow in her lap. Marie watched her move the brush with the dark red polish from the bottom to the top of each of her toenails.

"Is it hard to have two girls?" Marie asked. Crystal was quiet for a minute, concentrating on the polish. "It's hard when you're alone. When Donald passed away it was just me and the girls. My mom helped, you know, but it was just us."

"I didn't know he died."

"He overdosed when Shasta was six. Tawn was four. I just kept busy after that, you know. Had the girls in everything, dance, basketball, whatever. Cause every time I stopped, I had to think about it. As long as we were moving, it was okay."

"How'd you meet Keith?"

"We went to high school together. Then last year they put Etta in the hospital and I was working. The thing about Keith is, he loves my girls."

Marie watched Crystal move the polish brush. She watched her mouth pucker and felt the breath on her feet. Marie felt like she would melt. Like all the warmth of the bodies in that little house was concentrated around her. She felt loose and over-whelmed. "Crystal, I don't know if I can do this."

Crystal's eyes squinted a little. "Do what?"

"The baby. Everything."

It would never be that warm, there would never be a blanket with a picture of her baby on it telling her how much she was loved. She knew enough to understand she didn't know how to make that happen.

THE NEXT MORNING Marie woke up feeling better than she had in weeks. The girls were pouring cereal into bowls and Crystal was making coffee. Crystal took a shower. She tried to get Marie to stay but she was ready to go.

When they were in the car, Crystal asked her what she still needed for the baby. "Got a stroller yet?" Marie said no. "Car seat?" Marie shook her head. "Blankets? Bottles? Clothes?"

Marie's good feeling melted away.

When they got to Langdon Street, Marie felt like she was seeing Bobo's house for the first time. The cracked stucco. The sagging gutters. The weeds in what used to be a flower garden.

When they pulled into Bobo's driveway, Marie hesitated. She leaned over and gave Crystal a hug. "Thank you, Crystal. You really helped me." Marie grabbed her backpack and walked across the yard to Bobo's house.

TWENTY-THREE

MARIE DIDN'T SEE Bobo for two days. On the third day, she went to the dollar store and when she got back Bobo was there, working on a new project—covering the windows with aluminum foil. His eyes were red and his pupils were huge. He kept flexing his muscles and looking down at his biceps as he pulled the foil from the box and cut it off. He started covering the sliding glass door behind the table. He put a long section of foil against the glass, taped it down, then used the foil box to smooth it and keep it in place. It made Marie sick, him blocking the light from that window, blocking her view of the back yard.

"What are you doing?" she asked, even though it was obvious.

He kept running the edge of the box down along the window. "Security," he said, without looking at her.

Marie went to the bathroom. She turned the shower on to wash her hair. She took a long time with it, making sure to soap up every strand, making sure to rinse it all out. Then she put on the dollar store conditioner and rinsed that out. When she was done, she combed it all the way down to get out all the tangles. With the water off she could hear Bobo out in the living room, shearing off the foil on the hard sharp edge of the box. Marie opened the middle drawer of the bathroom cabinet and took out the scissors. She put them on the edge of the sink.

She heard Bobo say, "Office," and heard him put the key in the lock, and open the office door. She walked to the doorway and listened. She could hear him moving around. He opened the drawer of the file cabinet, unzipped the money bag. He opened and closed the drawer, opened and closed it again. He did that over and over, each time, getting louder. "That goddamned bunch of snakes. Bastards!" He slammed the drawer.

Marie stepped back into the bathroom and shut the door. She picked up the scissors, held her hair like it was in a ponytail right at the back of her neck, and cut straight across. She let the hair fall to the floor around her. She could still hear Bobo in the office, slamming things and cussing. When she got to the hair in the front of her head, she made herself some long bangs that came down past her eyebrows. She looked at herself in the mirror. She didn't look any better. Blonde, she decided, would look better on her short hair, she should make it blonde now.

Bobo opened the bathroom door. "What the hell?" He looked down at all the black hair on the floor, then looked at Marie. For a minute, he looked like he forgot why he was banging on the door. "You done anything with the money that was there in the office? In the file cabinet?"

She shook her head, she looked him right in the eye. "No," she said. "What money?"

"Bastards!" he said and he hit the door frame with his open palm. "Dammit!"

"What happened?" Marie asked.

"They took it. They come in here and acted like everything was all right. 'Oh let's have a party, Bobo,' like we was all big buddies, and they got in there and took that money." He hit the door frame again. Then he stopped talking and left.

Marie leaned over and started picking the hair up off the floor and putting it in the trash can. She heard Bobo call Nikki and leave a long message, blaming her and his brothers for taking the money from the office. Money that was to go to the store.

Then he dialed Keith. "You fucking shitball bastard," Bobo yelled into the phone. "Yes, you do know what I'm talking about. You think I wouldn't find out? What'd you think you'd do with it anyway?"

He slammed the phone down. "I mean, try and get ahead, try and do something to get us going here. Shit!" He kept yelling like he was talking to his brother. "Marie, get in here!"

She picked up the last of the big hunks of hair and put it in the trash can, and walked into the living room.

"Come on, you're going with me. I'm going to need a witness."

Marie got her purse from the bedroom then went to the kitchen. Bobo was getting one of his guns down from the kitchen cabinet above the refrigerator.

"Where are we going?" she asked, but she knew. "You're scaring me," she said.

"Some people around here need to be scared."

ON THE WAY out to Ed's place, Bobo was silent. Marie held onto the door of the Jeep with one hand. He drove so fast, took the turns at such speed it pushed and pulled her around on the seat. They passed the trailer. They passed Etta's house down in the bottom on the right, Carlos' house up on the left. They went up and down a rise in the road so quick that her stomach lurched.

Bobo steered into Ed's driveway with such a hard turn Marie thought she might throw up. He put the Jeep in park but left it running. "Come on," he said. Ed's car wasn't in the driveway, and there weren't any signs anybody was home.

"Bobo what are you going to do?" She followed him across the rocky yard.

"I'm going to get some answers." He took the porch steps two at a time, banged on the door with the side of his fist. "You better get your ass out here!" he yelled. He went around to the side of the house and looked in the windows. He went to the back and tried that door to see if it was open, but it wasn't. "Bastards," he said. He went back around to the porch and banged on the front door again.

"Well, no shit." He kicked the front door. He grabbed a clay flowerpot that was sitting on the porch rail. It had a dead plant in it. He held it with both hands and heaved it against the house. The black potting soil left a dark mark on the white siding, and the clay pieces and roots fell on the porch boards.

They got back in the Jeep and Bobo drove to Bert's house. "Stay here," he said to Marie, so she did. He turned the car off and took the keys with him. She watched him walk up to the porch. He was skeleton skinny now, he had no muscles, even though he tried to flex them all the time, especially his biceps. He moved all the time and never stopped. He was like a blur even as he stood talking with Bert on the porch. Bert would listen then ask Bobo a question. Bobo's arms kept going up, pointing back to Ed's place, then pointing toward town. He'd circle around on the porch, pace up and down. He kicked a post, but not that hard. Finally Bobo sat down on a porch step. Bert put his hand on his shoulder and said something. Bobo nodded.

He was calmer when they drove home, but that changed when they turned onto Langdon Street and saw Keith sitting in his car with the window down. He jerked the Jeep into park, jumped out of the driver's side. "You better be bringing me the money," Bobo yelled at him. "I'm not fucking kidding."

Keith opened the car door slow, and got out. "Bud, you think I'd come here to your house if I stole your money? Come on now. We both know who done this."

Bobo's head jerked, his whole body jerked, his mouth turned down. Bobo looked old to her, old but skinny, his pants sagging down, T-shirt like a pillow case hung on a twig, looking like it could start blowing, make enough of a sail to take Bobo away.

"Come on, now," Keith said. "If you and me fall out, this whole thing is going to go down the tubes. You know that."

"Well looks like we have," Bobo finally said.

"You remember when Daddy and Uncle Toddy and Uncle Larney got into it," Keith said. "Toddy threatened Larney with a tire iron. Remember? That was the end of that, all three of them working together. But then Daddy and Uncle Toddy, they picked back up and worked together. It didn't stop them two." Keith pulled out a cigarette and offered one to Bobo, and he took it. Keith squinted, blew out smoke. He looked like a person who had just rolled out of bed, his shorts rumpled, his gray T-shirt dirty looking.

"What I'm saying, Bobo, is that there is me, and there is you. Why we need anybody else, man? Come on. You know how to do this now. Fuck the money, we'll get that money back. When we get this shit going, we're not going to know what to do with all the money that'll be rolling in here. Then we can build up the outfitter business. We can do whatever we want 'cause we can. Motherfuck, Bobo. Let Ed have that damn money. He can have it, let him go."

Bobo was listening, not saying anything. Keith started to open the car door. "What about Nikki?" Bobo asked.

Keith let go of the door handle. "What about Nikki? She's probably took half the money. Ed probably gave her half."

Bobo shook his head. "I don't think so."

"All right. Well, maybe she can help," Keith said.

Bobo threw his cigarette down. "Screw Ed," he said.

Keith opened the door of his car and got into the driver's seat. "You let me know the next batch, I'll be out there. All right?"

Bobo leaned over into the window and said something to Keith that Marie couldn't hear.

She went inside and found a honey bun and ate it.

TWENTY-FOUR

B OBO, KEITH, AND BERT went to the store building and waited for Ed to show up. They were supposed to get together to frame the walls for the back office. Marie sat on the barstool beside the door and chewed the straw from a Slush Puppy.

"Can we go out on the river?" she asked Bobo.

He didn't answer. Maybe he didn't hear her. People sometimes didn't hear what she said. So she said it again. The second time he looked up at her with a nail in his mouth. "Can't you see I'm busy?" It sounded so mean. It sounded like there was hate underneath it, even though his voice was low. It was hard-edged with something Marie hadn't heard before.

Crystal came in with two buckets and cleaning supplies. She and Marie took the buckets to the bathroom in the back of the store and filled them with hot water from the sink. They started washing down the walls and the floors with rags dipped in the hot soapy water.

"Bobo, what color you going to paint these walls?" Crystal asked. He didn't answer. "I'm ready to paint."

"I'm not," Bobo said.

The door opened and Ed and Lynette walked in. Lynette had a dog with her. "This is Bruno," she said. "Ed got him for me. Ain't he cute?" She reached out and put her arm around Ed and leaned her head over on him. It was the first time Marie had seen Lynette smile. Keith bent down to pet the dog. The dog was wagging its tail so hard its feet were sliding around on the floor.

"Where'd you find him?" he asked Ed.

Lynette answered. "He was a stray." The dog licked Keith. "Oh, he likes you. That's a good boy, Bruno. Good dog!" She leaned over and petted him.

Crystal walked over to check Bruno out, so Marie did too.

"I've been wanting a dog," Crystal said. "I want a teacup poodle. You ever seen one? They cost three hundred dollars."

Bobo dropped something at the back of the store and the dog ran back to check him out. Bobo made no move to pet him. Lynette ran back to them, and the dog thought it was a game, so he ran from her, over to Marie and Crystal, then to another corner of the store. He hiked his leg and let out an amber stream Marie took in a sharp breath. Bobo saw it but he was silent.

"You know you can't pee inside, Bruno!" Lynette said. She grabbed his leash.

"Well, I'm here to put in my time." Ed plugged in a little radio he brought and put it on Crawford's AM station.

"No, that ain't right," Bobo said. He walked straight toward Ed. "You're not going to be putting any time in here. I guess you think I don't know you stole my fucking money."

"Hold up here, brother, hold up just a minute." It was Ed's turn now. "I didn't take any goddamned money from you. I don't have to steal from you. I know how to make money, and I taught you how to make money, how to cook, instead of doing all this silly piddlin' useless shit." His hands made billowy motions toward the walls and floor of the store. "We need to be working at the trailer on the stuff that matters. Who the hell is going to come to Pennington, the asshole of Larkin County, to rent a fucking canoe?"

Bobo and Ed were right up in each other's face now. Marie saw the nail gun at Bobo's feet, she saw nails spraying out of the gun and sticking into everyone there, nails going into people's eyes, into her belly. She made her way behind Bobo and picked it up. The brothers didn't notice.

Bobo poked Ed's chest. "You agreed to this, remember? When I came back from Indiana we sat down, and you agreed."

"Get your finger off my chest."

Bobo poked again.

"I didn't agree to this. I don't need this bullshit. I got my own business to take care of. And get your fucking finger off me."

"No," Bobo said, then Ed hit Bobo with his fist, hard. Bobo's head snapped back. Keith moved in to stop it, but before he could, Bobo hit Ed in the mouth and they started wailing on each other and were just a blur. Bert tried to break it up but he got punched.

"Stop it!" Crystal screamed. The dog started growling, pulling at his leash. Even Lynette was yelling at them to stop.

Bobo hit Ed again. Ed toppled over.

"You did not just do that!" Lynette screamed to Bobo. She picked up a two-by-four and hit Bobo right under his ribs and he went down on his hands and knees.

"Motherfuck!" he said.

Lynette stood over him with the two-by-four gripped like a softball bat aimed right at his head. "You better believe it."

While he was still down, Bobo held up his hand. "Get them out of here," he said to Bert. "Get them all out of here."

MARIE EASED her arm under Bobo and helped him off the floor. His face was twisted in pain and he held his side.

"Do you need to go to the hospital?" Bert asked.

"Just get me home."

"I'll help you," Marie said. They walked slow across the store. Bobo made little whimpering noises. "It'll be okay," she said.

Bert and Marie helped Bobo into the Jeep. His mouth was swollen and one of his eyes was bright red, looked hot to the touch. He cussed as he twisted his body in the seat. "Get the nail gun and lock up," he told Marie as he leaned back onto the headrest. Marie shut the Jeep door. She walked to the back of the store to turn off the lights. Their cleaning buckets and supplies were still on the floor. There were drops of blood where the fight had been. She hoped Bobo had broken Ed's nose. She switched the breaker and the lights went out. At the front of the store she stood for a minute, looking through the window at Bobo in the car. He looked smaller. His eyes were closed. It scared her. She grabbed the nail gun and locked the door.

At home, she put bags of ice wrapped in towels on his face and side. He let her run him a warm bath, help him down into the green bathtub. She looked at his body in the water, so small and pale and naked. Now with a big red mark on his side that would soon enough be black and blue, his face a swollen mess. She touched him on the top of his head, a place he probably wasn't hurting, and just kept her hand there. He closed his eyes.

"There's money to be made there, I know it."

"I'll help you," she said.

He opened his eyes, shook his head. "We all agreed."

"You keep saying that but you're the only one of them who seems to care." She stayed with him until his pain started to ease a little. Her feet were falling asleep underneath her.

Marie could see her purpose. She would be the one to help Bobo. She would take care of him. She would take care of their baby. She would help him make Owens Outfitters happen. She would make the whole back yard a garden.

PART FOUR

TWENTY-FIVE

MARIE STOOD in the back yard, looking down at the spot where she had buried the money under the flowers. The first thing she would buy with the money would be a crib. A nice one, made out of real wood. Something solid. And a nice set of sheets and blankets. And a stroller and car seat. All those things the baby would need. If there was enough left over she'd buy some pretty baby clothes, little white cotton dresses and black shiny shoes. She would tell everyone her parents gave her the money, or that they bought it for her outright. She imagined her mom calling, imagined her mom's voice over the phone telling her she was going to take her shopping for the baby.

Marie heard a noise and looked up from the ground. Nikki opened the sliding glass door and walked out onto the patio. "Bobo ever show up?"

"Yep," Marie answered.

Nikki kept her sunglasses on and walked toward Marie. She wore a denim miniskirt and a lace shirt that looked like it had been made from a tablecloth. "Where the hell was he?"

Marie shook her head.

Nikki looked down at the ground. "What happened here?"

Marie told her about the bulbs she'd planted, the bulbs Etta gave her. She had a strange and sudden urge to tell Nikki about the money. She bit her lip to keep her mouth shut.

"Where is Bobo now?" Nikki asked.

"He left at four this morning. I haven't seen him since. I didn't know where he was coming from, and I don't know where he was going."

"Makes two of us. Well, I'm ready to roll on this next batch. Tell him that when you see him."

Marie was shaky after Nikki left. She didn't feel right. Like her body was not under her control. She went inside, made some tea, and sat down on the couch. She couldn't stand the noise from the radio or TV so she left them off. She leaned her head back and propped her feet up on the coffee table. She couldn't sit that way for long though, she needed to move. She paced the living room in her bare feet then put shoes on and went outside to sit on the landing.

Bobo pulled in, driving slow. It took him ten minutes, it seemed like, to get out of the Jeep and walk across the yard. He didn't say anything as he passed her and went into the house. She followed him inside. He sat down at the table and she sat down in a chair across from him. One strip of foil still hung on the sliding glass door behind him. He put his head in his hands. Marie didn't know what to say, so she just sat, waiting.

"It's done with my brothers." He rubbed his eyes. When he moved his hands away the skin around his eyes looked raw, and everything that should've been white was red. "Bert's out of money. But I got a plan. This is going to happen."

IT WAS TOO hard to be around Bobo when he was this way, so Marie went to the park to walk. Crawford Park was only a couple of blocks away from Bobo's house, and it had a walking track that went all the way around. Each lap was a quarter of a mile.

The park was nothing great. It was down in a bowl beside the quarry and had an amphitheater. Marie walked by a couple of kids mounding sand in the playground. She saw a wadded-up latex glove in the grass beside a trash can. She looped around down by the wooded area, where she could see the houses along Quarry Street. Four or five middle school boys sat on the back wall of the amphitheater. A BMX bike leaned against the wall and one of the boys kept moving the handlebars back and forth.

When Marie got close enough, she said hey and they said hey back to her. Then she said, "How are you all doing?" She heard her dad in her voice then, heard her dad acknowledging people, talking to people that he saw, whether he knew them or not. "Doing all right," one of the boys said.

As she walked around the curve of the walking track, she heard a girl on the grassy stage that probably had never been used for a play. The girl yelled that she needed a motherfucking lighter for her goddamned cigarette. Two boys standing beside her searched their pockets. Marie watched the girl. She was twelve, maybe thirteen. She wore a push-up bra under her printed tank top, shiny white basketball shorts that came down to her knees, and knock-off Air Jordans with hot pink soles.

Marie kept walking. She walked by the train tracks that rose up ten or fifteen feet above the park. The tracks came out of the quarry and circled round to make part of the bowl that formed the park. When she got to the playground again, the girl was riding one of the bikes around. She had blue-green hair. Everyone in the park watched her. The couples who sat on top of the picnic tables under the shelter watched her. Some older girls and a boy on the basketball court watched her. She was like a magnet, even Marie couldn't help herself.

The girl moved to the swings and the boys followed her and all of them swung for a while. When she jumped off the swing, her small body floated in the air, hair flowed behind, until she landed on her knees and jumped back up.

The girl got back on the bike. One of the boys followed her. They rode across the basketball court, through the half-court game the older girls played. The girl turned so sharp at the midcourt line she made the boy wreck into her, their bikes made a metal tangle on the concrete, the boy momentarily underneath it all. The girl stood up unhurt and laughed down at the boy.

Then Marie saw the blue and yellow of the CSX engine, up above all of them, as it moved out of the quarry. The cars on the train were weirdly new, weirdly clean and unscratched, all painted the same dark brown color with white letters on the side. They were full of gravel. She'd never seen numbers and letters that clear and crisp on the side of a train.

The train was moving slow and when the horn sounded all the people in the park put their fingers in their ears, but not that girl. It was like her already amped-up body got another spark lit in it. She grabbed the boy's arm and they ran through the grass, past the picnic shelters, through the sand of the playground area, up the scrubby hill to the tracks, right up to the moving train.

They stood so close to the train, it made Marie clench her fists. She fought the urge to yell at her to get back down and away from there. She willed the girl back down the hill, back into the bowl of the park. But the girl didn't come back. She started to run beside a car and grabbed one of the metal bars that went up the side of the car like a ladder. She stood on one bar and held onto another until she disappeared from view.

Part of Marie wanted to grab that same bar and be up there with her, moving on down the track to wherever that train was going. Somewhere far away. She thought of how they could fall under those neat new wheels, under those neat new cars, all the weight of that gravel would push down on them, and the wheels would cut their bodies in half, let one half roll down the hill into some other park in some other town along the rail line, the other half roll down onto the highway. It would be quick. She was beginning to see the benefit of a quick death.

Marie sat on a bench where she could watch the rest of the cars roll by. The boy who had followed the girl acted like he was going to jump on the train too, but it was moving faster now. He stood back from the tracks and threw gravel at the last car on the train, then he jogged behind it down the track.

The girl must have hung on only as far as downtown Crawford because she came running back down the tracks, back down the scrubby hill into the park, back among the boys who were still sitting in the amphitheater. They were all loud now, the boys and this girl, sitting in the grass with their bikes beside them.

A police car pulled up. Marie heard the girl say, "Oh shit," and then saw her jump the fence of the track and take off through the trees. Marie watched her run up Quarry Street, run across a yard, and disappear into a small white house. The police officer talked to the boys and Marie tried to listen, to see what he was asking them. The boys were talking low, but she heard one of them say, "She went to my mammaw's house."

Marie wondered if she should have made the call to the police. She was old enough now to be someone's mother, she could be the mother of that girl someday. Maybe her baby, her daughter, would grow up to be that wild, that dangerous.

TWENTY-SIX

THE NEXT DAY, Bobo was ready to go to work on his plan. He said they had to go to Etta's and he wanted Marie to drive. "So why am I going?" she asked. Bobo wouldn't look at her. "I don't care," she said. "I just want to know."

He rubbed his mouth and coughed. "She might give me the money if you're with me."

"What am I supposed to say?"

"Don't say anything. Let me handle it." He put his hand on the notebook and said, "I got it all planned out."

Marie kept her eyes on the road, hands on the wheel. When Etta's house came into view, she turned off the road and onto the gravel driveway.

Etta sat on the couch in her living room with a big bowl of popcorn in her lap, watching *Wheel of Fortune* on TV. Marie almost went to the kitchen to get her own bowl, the popcorn looked and smelled so good, but then she remembered what they were there for, and that Bobo had told her to sit and keep her mouth shut, so she did.

Etta didn't raise her head when they came in. Bobo bent over to kiss her forehead and put his hand on her shoulder.

"Well, now," she said.

Marie sat on the love seat across from Etta and Bobo sat down with her. He held the notebook with his hand on one leg, the leg that kept bouncing up and down. Marie wondered if he'd done that in the bank when they wouldn't give him the money.

"Get you a Coke in there, if you want it," Etta said to Marie.

"Thanks, I'm okay."

Bobo started. "Etta, you know I got this plan, right? I got this building, I mean we bought this building down in Pennington. And I got some canoes, and some supplies. Trying to make a go of this business, this outfitter business." Marie noticed the sweat on Bobo's forehead. "So what we want to do, is take people down to the river, let them canoe, let them kayak, and then pick them up, bring them back to the store in Pennington." His words were coming out fast. The TV game show wheel kept clicking. The category for the puzzle appeared on the bottom of the screen: BEFORE AND AFTER.

"Yeah, I've heard of it," Etta said.

Bobo leaned forward. His leg was bobbing. "Well, what we need, what we got to have to make a go of this, are a couple vans. Now I've shopped around and the best deal I could get was down in Middlesboro. Two used vans." He opened the notebook and pulled out some papers he'd printed from the Internet. The papers had his writing on them where he'd talked to someone over the phone. He stood up and held out the papers for Etta to look at. Marie could see the sores on his forearms.

"So here's the problem. I don't have that kind of money saved up right now. I spent money on lumber to fix up the building. I spent money on equipment and canoes and kayaks." Etta looked at the paper he held out, but not for very long. "These vans, they're GMC and they're in good shape."

"Mmhmm."

"So, I've got a thousand on hand. I been to the car lot. They won't loan me anything except at twenty-three percent interest or something." He sat back down on the love seat beside Marie.

Etta moved her neck back and forth like it was hurting her. She leaned back on the couch. Someone knocked at the door. She put the bowl on the floor and stood up, stretched her back and walked slow to the door and opened it. The person who knocked stood back away from the door and to the side so he couldn't be seen from the inside. Etta talked to him, then went to the back bedroom and got a fifth of vodka, and probably some pills, then went back to the door. The man gave her cash, and she put it in the pocket of her housedress. She sat back down on the couch and put the popcorn bowl back on her lap.

Bobo didn't say anything. He looked sick and unhappy. The audience on the game show cheered.

"So what exactly are you wanting?" Etta finally said after she finished another mouthful of popcorn.

"Well, I guess I'm asking to borrow some money. The only reason I'm asking you, is cause we need these vans now. If we're going to make a go of it, we got to do it now."

Etta took in a deep breath. "If you'd done what I wanted, you'd had plenty of money."

Bobo's leg stopped moving.

"If you'd set up those pill runs to Williams County like I asked you to, like we agreed, then you'd had all kinds of money."

Bobo looked down and away from Etta, almost at Marie but not quite. "Number one," he said, "you never asked. You told. Number two, I couldn't make enough for gas money by the time I had to give you your share or your commission or whatever it was you called it." His muscles were tense in the back of his neck and one foot tapped some weird rhythm. He ran his hand through his hair. The TV wheel clicked and a contestant lost his turn after landing on the bankrupt slot.

"That stuff you're trying to peddle is not going to turn a profit. Anybody could look at that and see. No money in it."

Marie wasn't sure which business Etta was talking about.

"Your plan's not going to work, is what I'm saying." Her face didn't change. It hadn't changed since Bobo and Marie came in.

"All right," Bobo said.

"Foolishness," Etta said. It seemed like the end of things there, but she kept talking, even though Bobo stood up. "All you seem to be doing is putting your profits up your nose or in your arm."

"All right then," he said, notebook curled in his hand.

"You listen to what I'm saying. None of that stuff you're doing is going to come to any good end."

"Bunch of bullshit," Bobo said as he moved out the door. Marie glanced at Etta and then she followed Bobo outside.

TWENTY-SEVEN

T HE VOICE on the phone said, "I'm calling for Marie Massey."
Marie waited a second before she said anything back.

"Yeah, this is Marie."

"Marie, my name is Ann Lightfoot. I'm a prosecutor here in
Walters. I'm working on this case about your teacher, Jill Anglin."

Marie kicked herself for answering. "Yeah, okay."

"You might remember me, I'm a friend of your parents, been
a friend of theirs for a long time."

"Yeah, I remember you."

"You've been subpoenaed for the grand jury tomorrow."

Marie didn't say anything.

"You there?"

"Yeah, I'm here."

"I'd like to ask you some questions."

Marie thought of excuses. She had to go to the doctor. She was going to have her baby tomorrow. Finally she just said, "I've got to go."

"Marie, I've been hearing things about Ms. Anglin, that she's been trying to scare you about the grand jury. Is that right? Did she tell you not to give testimony tomorrow?"

"I've got to go."

"That's not right. That's another crime, intimidating a witness."

"Is my mom going to testify?"

"Yes."

"I've got to go now."

"You're subpoenaed for ten o'clock tomorrow. You can either talk to me now, and make it a little easier on yourself, or just show up then. You saw Ms. Anglin give your brother drugs, is that right?"

Marie didn't say anything.

"You're going to have to answer that at some point."

"Bye," Marie said, and hung up.

THE NEXT MORNING at eight there was a red car in the driveway and someone was knocking. Marie opened the door to see Kyle standing there in khaki pants and a button-down shirt.

"I'm here to take you to the courthouse."

"No, you're not."

"Yeah, I am."

"No."

"I'm— You are not going to jail over this," he said.

"They're not going to put me in jail."

"Yes, they are. They told me. If you don't show up they'll get the judge to put you in jail. So get ready."

She stepped back so Kyle could come into the house. "Okay, fine, but I've got to take a shower." She handed him the remote.

Marie got ready and Kyle watched TV. Then they got into his car and he drove them to Walters. When they pulled into the parking lot, Marie thought she would throw up. He parked right next to the building.

"Can you park on the other side, over there away from everything?" she asked.

He put the key back in the ignition and started it up, went to the parking spot she'd pointed to. "You okay?" he asked.

"Yeah. Great."

"You sure? You don't look so great."

"I really don't want to go in there."

He looked at her. "Better than jail though. You'll be okay. Makinley's in there, I'll be there. It'll be okay."

It felt good to sit in Kyle's front seat and talk, like they used to. She wanted to tell him all the crazy stuff going on in Crawford. She wanted to unload every last bit of it, let it all out.

"You know Ms. Anglin asked me out when we were dating."

Marie's stomach lurched.

"That's why they want me to testify here."

Ms. Anglin was, used to be, her friend. Marie told her things. She told her about Kyle, even told her what they did and what it was like. "Did you go out with her?"

"Hell no," he said.

Marie felt sick. Hearing that didn't make her want to be there any more than before. She started to cry.

Kyle patted her hand and she took hold of his hand before he could move it away. He squeezed her fingers. "Come on."

They opened the car doors and walked together to the side door of the building, and went inside.

THE WITNESSES were in one room, some kind of filing room with old olive-colored file cabinets. Marie sat down beside Kyle.

"Hello, Marie." Her mom sat in the corner in the only leather chair in the room. She wore a navy pantsuit, and had a newspaper in her lap.

"Hello," Marie said.

Makinley came in then and sat on the other side of Kyle. She looked nervous. Everyone in the room looked nervous, except Marie's mom. "Hello, Mrs. Massey," Makinley said.

Her mom stood up. "Marie, can I speak with you? Out here?" She opened the door and held it open until Marie stood up. Marie went through the door and into the hallway. Her mom looked up and down the hall then pointed to a little alcove with a water fountain. She walked ahead of Marie and turned when they reached it. Marie looked at her mother's lapel pin. It said Shane Massey Memorial Scholarship Fund in tiny raised letters.

"How far along are you?"

"About seven months."

"Have you been to the doctor?"

"No," Marie said. "Where's Dad?" She could hardly get the words out.

"He's not here." Her mom looked away. When she looked back, Marie was crying. Marie wiped the tears with her fingers, then wiped her hands on her dress.

"Come on, you'll be all right," her mom said.

Marie breathed deep and tried to get hold of herself, but couldn't. She walked to the bathroom. She went into a stall and locked the door. She heard her mother's heels on the tile floor, heard her stop in front of the stall. "You in there?" her mother said, knuckles hitting the metal door.

"Yeah." Marie was trying to wipe her nose.

"All you have to do today is tell the truth. Tell them everything you know about that woman. Everything she did to Shane. All the parties and the drugs. Everything. I know what happened and it wasn't right. It was criminal."

"I don't want to be here. Why are you doing this?"

"This is one last thing we can do for him. And then, when this is done, we can talk about what we're going to do about you."

"I'm scared," Marie put her palm on the stall door. "Things are really bad."

Her mom said nothing. Marie felt like she could taste the green paint and the metal, like the taste was coming through her hand on the door to the back of her throat.

"All you have to do is go in there and tell the truth. That is all you have to do. Tell the truth."

This woman is my mother and she cannot see me or hear me, Marie thought. She opened the door of the stall.

"Shane was going to go off and not ever come back. He told me. He hated it at home. He couldn't wait to get away from you and dad. Neither could I." She walked to the sink and splashed cold water on her face, then she left the bathroom and walked down the hall, her mom's heels clicking behind her.

Before she opened the door to the witness room, her mom grabbed her by the elbow. "You have no idea what this is like. You have no idea what it is like to lose a son. And I hope you never have to find out."

Marie looked in her mom's eyes. When she was small, she wanted to look as pretty as her mom, look so pretty that people's eyes would follow her. She tried to copy everything her mom did, wore the same makeup, ate the same food, did exercise videos with her. She even copied the way her mom talked about Shane, told people about his tournaments and his championships. When Marie was older, she helped in the office, filing papers, making copies. She heard a conversation between her mom and the receptionist. They were talking about their children, talking about how different their children were from each other. The receptionist had a girl and boy, they were small. The girl was always moving, always into something, her boy was more content, liked to play quietly by himself. Marie only half listened until her mom said, "Some of your children just need more from you than others. Shane, I don't know if it's because he's more talented or what, but he needs more from me than Marie ever will." Marie sat down, tried to make sure she had heard the words right. Then she stood up, threw the papers down, walked past her mom and slammed the door. From then on, she didn't do anything she thought her mother wanted her to do. What was the point.

MARIE WALKED on into the witness room. It wasn't like she could argue with her mom about how hard it was to lose a son. It wasn't like she hadn't seen what it did to their family. There was nothing more to say. She sat down next to Kyle. He was looking at his watch and whispering to Makinley. A couple teachers were grading papers. Principal Ashmore went in and out of the room. Ten o'clock came and went. Marie got queasy. She hadn't eaten and she didn't have money for the vending machines. She asked Makinley for some change, but she didn't have any. She asked Kyle. She felt like she was going to throw up as he handed her two dollars from his wallet. Her hands were clammy. "You okay?" he asked.

"Yeah, I'm fine. I'm going to find some peanut butter crackers." She went to the basement on the elevator, found the vending machine and put her money in. She put the rest of the money in the Coke machine. She sat on a bench outside the sheriff's office. Deputies went in and out of the glass door with the gold star on it. She licked the salt off one of the crackers then ate it.

Marie finished the crackers and pop, but stayed there on the bench. After a while the elevator doors opened and Makinley stepped out. "They called your mom in, and Kyle. They said I'll be next." They got on the elevator together and rode up in silence.

The doors opened on the second floor and Marie took a quick breath in. Ms. Anglin, twenty pounds heavier than the last time she saw her, was standing there. Her face was blotchy and her faded blonde hair had two-inch black roots. A man in a suit guided her toward the hallway. "I guess we're going this way," she said. She looked back at Makinley and Marie. "Sure was good to see you all." And then she was gone.

"She looks like shit," Makinley said.

Back in the witness room, Kyle came in and they called Makinley. "All that and they asked me four questions," he whispered to Marie. "Yours probably won't take long either." He was trying to make her feel better.

"Thanks for the money," she whispered back.

"No problem." They were quiet for a minute. "We miss you. At school, I mean. Me and Makinley."

Marie nodded. If she looked at him, she would cry, so she didn't. "I keep thinking if Shane was here, he would've figured a way to get out of this. He wouldn't be sitting here like we are, waiting to be called. I can't figure out how he always did that."

"He didn't have to," Kyle said. "He had your mom."

When Kyle said that, she felt better. She didn't know anyone else could see how their family worked.

Makinley came back into the room, which was getting stuffy and stale as the day wore on. "They want you," she said to Marie. She thought about what she would say about Ms. Anglin. But it didn't matter. It was already over. Ms. Anglin was over.

215

TWENTY-EIGHT

AFTER THE VISIT to Etta's, Bobo left and didn't come back. When he had been gone for six days, Marie got down to her last ten dollars. She made lunch and looked at the can of beef ravioli, which would be her supper. That night she would have to dig up the money under the flowers. She would wait until dark to do it. In the meantime, it was Thursday and the newspaper had come out and she wanted to read it, and she wanted to look at blonde hair dye, so she walked to the drugstore in town.

She picked up *The Crawford Call* and read it in the aisle. She read the first paragraphs of the article on the front page about a four-county drug bust, then turned to the middle page where it was continued.

"You're looking mighty ripe." Ed's loud voice came from right in front of her. She hadn't seen him come in. She kept reading.

He smacked the paper down and the pages ripped right down the middle.

"Shit, now I've got to buy this thing," Marie said, trying to fold it back up the way it came.

Then Ed was up in her face, right up where the paper had been. "I didn't take the fucking money," he said. "You be sure and tell him that. You understand?" He was standing so close, and whispering, but loud enough for anyone in the store to hear. "You keep yourself safe over there, all alone. You never know who might be watching you, little sister."

"Fuck off, Ed." Marie managed to push past him. Two cashiers stood next to the register watching them. Marie took the torn newspaper and put down fifty cents on the counter as she walked by. She went out the back way, past the magazines and down a short dark hall to the back entrance, down some concrete steps and into the small parking lot. She walked across the street, down the hill and across the train tracks, back to Bobo's house.

Marie got out the gun Bobo kept in their bedroom on the shelf in the closet above their clothes. It was loaded, like all the other guns in the house, but she got the box of ammo down too. She kept the gun pointed down as she walked. She kept it with her wherever she went in the house that day, careful to keep it pointed away from her on the table or on the chair next to her. She didn't have a pocket that could hold it, and she was afraid it would go off in her pocket anyway.

Before it got dark, she got the shovel out of the garage and set it on the back patio. She put Bobo's blue flashlight there too and made sure it worked. She listened to the Crawford AM radio station as she cleaned up the kitchen. Then she made some lemonade and sat out on the patio, gun on the table beside her, waiting for dark.

As the sun was going down, Marie walked around the edge of the yard, peered down into bushes and over the back fence to make sure Ed wasn't there somewhere. She went around the front of the house too, careful to hold the gun so no one could see it. She checked between the garbage cans on the side of the house, went through the garage, watched the traffic on the street to make sure he wasn't driving by and watching. She convinced herself he was nowhere around. She waited on the patio until it was dark enough that she could dig without being seen

It was hard to hold the shovel and the flashlight and the gun with two hands. She put the shovel in the crook of her right arm, held the flashlight in that same hand, gun in the other, and stepped off the patio. She heard a noise around the side of the house and she stopped dead still. It was footsteps.

"Who's there?" She dropped the shovel and the flashlight in the grass and moved the gun to her right hand.

"Hey Marie." It was Keith, walking toward her in the dark.

Marie took a deep breath. "Hey Keith." She turned on the patio light, sat down on one of the metal chairs and slipped the gun on the low table beside it. If Keith noticed the gun he didn't say anything. He pulled over a plastic chair and sat next to her. Neither of them talked or looked at the other.

He breathed deep and coughed, and leaned his chair back. "How you holding up?"

"Okay, I guess."

He threw his head back a little, a sort of nod. "You know, Crystal and I were talking about you." He lit a cigarette. "We were thinking we could help you out with that baby."

"What do you mean?"

"We could help you, you know, keep it some, or whatever." The second he said those words, there was a snap and a back leg of the plastic chair buckled and broke under his weight, and he went down with a thud on his back. He rolled on one side, moaning. Marie waited a minute before she asked if he was okay. He put his hand to the back of his head, then pulled it away. It had blood on it.

"Shit," he said. "Stone cold sober and can't even sit in a chair." He laughed a little, still on the ground. He put his hand back to his head again and got to his knees. Marie could see the blood oozing between his fingers. She went inside for paper towels. When she came back out he was sitting on the edge of the patio.

"Here." She handed him some paper towels. She tore off some more and put them down to soak up the blood on the patio.

"Damn, this thing is bleeding." He pulled away the towels and Marie gave him some more. "Thanks," he said. The Rottweilers next door got riled up. When they quieted down, Keith said, "I mean, you can do what you want."

"About what, Keith?"

"We'd keep the baby for you. If that was what you wanted."

"You mean babysit?"

"Yeah that, or just, you know, keep it. Raise it for you." He pressed the towels a little tighter against the back of his head.

"Why are you talking about this?"

"It's just, me and Crystal been talking. I don't know. You're young, and Bobo is Bobo. We just wanted to tell you that. You know, if you needed that, we would help." A door opened on one of the houses on the street, and some kids screamed out, then everything was quiet again. "You don't have to say nothing, just think about it," he said. And he left.

THE NEXT MORNING the phone started ringing early and it woke Marie up. Nobody else was home to answer. Nobody else was home anymore, except her, and she was always there. Getting fatter. Growing in the belly, swelling in the limbs. She rolled herself off Bobo's side of the bed. Didn't matter, so she slept all over the bed now, sprawled out.

When she answered, a girl's voice came through. A familiar girl. "Marie?"

"Yeah, who's this?"

A pause. "Me, dumbass." It was Makinley.

Marie hardly recognized the voice, even though it hadn't been that long. Nothing around Marie seemed real, nothing back in Caudill was real either.

"Hey," Marie said.

"That thing about Ms. Anglin— she's in jail now. I think she made some kind of deal. Thought you'd want to know. Had you heard?"

"No," Marie said. She started picking dirty clothes up off the floor and throwing them up on the bed. "Okay, well thanks for calling." She was out of breath from moving around.

"Your dad moved out." Makinley said it like she was enjoying it. Like it made her happy somehow.

Marie stopped and sat down on the bed. She had no need to discuss this with her former best friend. "All right. See you around."

"Are you coming back?" Makinley asked before Marie could hang up.

"Coming back where?"

"My parents said you could live with us, if you want."

The only thing worse than living with her own parents would be living with Makinley's parents. Marie told her goodbye and hung up the phone and laid back down.

TWENTY-NINE

MARIE WORKED all that day on the attic room, making it ready for the baby. She carried boxes out to the garage, swept and dusted. She washed an old curtain she found in a dresser and put it up over the window. When she was finished, she had a dark empty room that she still didn't want to put a baby in.

She set the alarm for three a.m. and fell asleep as soon as it got dark. She stayed asleep for a few hours, until her whole body jerked awake. When she tried to go back to sleep, her body kept her from it, legs or arms jerking.

Her eyes opened every fifteen minutes. Each time she looked at the alarm clock, something different bothered her. At one fifteen, she wanted the old Bobo back. She imagined him lost somewhere down on the river. If she went there, maybe she could find him. If she climbed up in a tree, she could watch for a while then jump down into his canoe when he floated by. And they could start all over again. At one thirty, she wondered where he really was. In someone else's house, she knew. Probably down in Wayne County with some woman who smelled good and wore tight clothes and had a boat. Maybe they were driving around in her Alfa Romeo, and maybe they had crashed on some back road and they were bleeding right now, dying alone. At one forty-five, she had to get up because her heartburn was so bad. She went to the kitchen and got the Tums out of the cabinet. She paced in a circle around the kitchen table. How was she going to do this. She didn't know how to make a bottle. She didn't know how to change a diaper. She still had nothing a baby would need except a dark nursery. She'd never really been around a baby. She didn't know what to do with a baby.

She drank some water and went back to bed. When she closed her eyes, she saw a pink baby blanket. She opened it, knowing her baby was there, but all she could see were tiny pink baby feet, not attached to anything else. They didn't even have shoes on.

Then she knew it was time, and she got out of the bed. She grabbed the towel from the bathroom that was stained with hair dye and the flashlight from the kitchen. She opened the door to the patio and put on her muddy shoes. The shovel was where she had left it. She took all this into the back yard.

She laid the towel beside the spot where the money was buried. She pushed the shovel down into the ground. The first thing she'd buy would be paint for the upstairs room. Maybe that would lighten it up. She stopped and looked around the dark yard. Bobo hadn't been home for days, but she thought she heard something. She pushed the shovel down again and started shoveling dirt out of the hole. The flashlight didn't help, she couldn't hold it and dig at the same time so she put it down, and it just shined straight across the ground. She wished someone was there to shine it down where she was digging.

The next thing she'd buy would be the crib. She shoveled out all the bulbs she had planted, then dug down to the bottom of the hole where she had buried the plastic IGA bag with the money. She reached down and pulled the bag out. She held it for a minute, shook the dirt off and laid it on the towel next to her. The third thing she'd buy would be a car seat. She refilled the hole with the loose dirt and bulbs, wrapped the towel around the bag and picked it up. She held it against her body, and carried the shovel and flashlight in the other hand. She put the shovel down on the patio and took her shoes off, and opened the sliding glass door.

"What have we here?" Bobo said from the dark. Marie dropped the towel-wrapped bag and the flashlight on the floor. A little trickle of pee ran down her leg. She picked up the flashlight but pushed the bag under the table with her foot. She shined the light toward the voice, toward the living room. Even in the weak light she could see that Bobo's eyes were red, his face skeletal. He squinted, put his hand over his eyes.

"Get that off of me," he said. Marie kept the flashlight on him, but when he stood up she switched it off. He turned the living room light on.

"Where you been?" she asked him.

"Never mind. I been taking care of business." He sat back down in the chair beside the TV, crossed his legs and laced his fingers together in front of his stomach, elbows on the armrests. "I got a better question. What the hell are you doing?"

Marie took a deep breath. "You've been gone for six days and that's all you got? Taking care of business? That's bullshit."

"Free country last time I checked." He said such stupid stuff now. She rolled her eyes. "What's that you kicked up under the table?" he asked.

Marie didn't answer.

He stood up and started toward her. "I asked you a question."

Marie reached for the bag, trying to keep the towel wrapped around it. She wanted to get away but she knew she'd never be able to outrun him.

"And why the hell are you digging up whatever it is in the back yard in the middle of the night?" He stood across the kitchen table from her.

"You're full of shit, Bobo."

He nodded, eyes closed. "Answer the question."

"And you don't even care that the baby is coming."

The house was so quiet at that hour.

"I never asked for a baby."

"I never asked for you to be a drug dealer and sleep around with whores," Marie said, the towel-wrapped bag trembling in her hands.

"Well I guess we neither one have got what we wanted here," he said.

"I guess not."

"What's in the towel?" He moved around the corner of the table. "What's in it?" His voice was harder this time and he was right up next to her. He pulled the towel and bag from her. The towel fell away. He tore open the plastic and dumped the Ziploc bags onto the table.

Marie's hand tightened on the flashlight.

"Well, well," he said, looking at the bags. "I guess we know where this came from." His mouth barely moved over the words. He touched each bag with his fingertips. "Guess we know exactly what this is and where it came from." He moved closer to her, every muscle in his body tightened, his hands clenched. She raised the flashlight to hit him before he could hit her, but he grabbed her arm and knocked her across the temple with the flashlight in her own hand. She took a sharp breath in. He didn't let go of her and hit her with the flashlight again. He twisted her arm back until she screamed.

"That hurts!"

"That's the point," he said. His breath was on her and she wouldn't look at his eyes. All she could see were his teeth, a couple of them almost black in places. She couldn't twist away from his grip. She dropped the flashlight and it fell with a thump onto the floor.

"You should have gone home a long time ago."

"I had to take it, Bobo. The baby needs stuff and you don't even care. You don't even want this baby."

"You should've just gone on back to your momma and your big-ass house."

"She doesn't want me!" She was screaming now, and crying.

"You've made me blame my brothers, my own flesh and blood, for something you did."

He picked up the money and took it into the office. He came back and pushed the lever down to lock the glass door. He pushed the kitchen table until it butted up against the glass.

Marie tried to run to the front door but she wasn't fast enough, he moved in front of her easily, pushed her out of his way. "Nope," he said, and he locked the front door too. He heaved against the couch and moved it across the living room to block that door. He made sure the windows were locked then got the boxes of tin foil from the kitchen cabinet, left over from his first attempt to cover all the windows.

CARRIE MULLINS

Marie sat down on one of the kitchen chairs that had no table now. Her head was pounding and her arm hurt. Bobo was moving in fast-forward, never stopping, motions jerky and speeded up as he went window to window. He kept all the foil on the same side, dull side facing in, until the windows were silvered. "You're going to stay in for a while, until we get this figured out," he said.

Marie went to the bedroom and got in bed. In her dream that night the baby had a body. It was sitting on the bough of a pine tree in her grandma's back yard. It was pink and naked. It sat still. She couldn't figure how a little baby could sit in a tree, how it could stay on the branch without falling. She moved toward it, then ran toward it, but when she got to the tree the baby disappeared. She looked up, into the higher branches, and down at the brown pine needles underneath, but the baby was gone.

THIRTY

THE NEXT MORNING Marie spotted the small bag of white stuff on the coffee table. It was the size of her thumb. She looked at it like she wasn't pregnant. She looked at it and even moved toward it, one step. She was trapped and she probably wouldn't even live long enough to have her baby. What would it hurt. She could just dissolve for a while. Just forget where she was, forget being miserable locked and tin-foiled up in Bobo's house.

Bobo walked out of the kitchen with something in his hand and sat down on the couch. The couch was still blocking the front door, the coffee table in front of it, like everything was normal, like the couch should be pushed up against the front door. Bobo opened the bag and tapped the white powder out onto the table. He lined it into three rows with his driver's license. When he put the straw at the end of the row, Marie looked away.

She went to the attic room. He hadn't foiled that window closed. She thought she could open it, at least get some air, but he followed her and made her come back down. Then he nailed the attic door shut. He followed her the rest of the day, yelling about how everyone was plotting against him, trying to poison him.

The phone rang and Marie ran for it, but Bobo beat her there. "Who's this?" he said into the receiver. He listened for a minute then said, "I don't have time to talk to you right now." It had to be Crystal, it was the time of day she usually called.

BOBO COULDN'T STAND the sounds coming out of the TV, so Marie stayed in the bedroom reading the old *Reader's Digest* again. She looked for baby names but none of them sounded right. She used one of Bobo's old notebooks and wrote down the first name of every person she had ever met. She drew circles around ten of them, all of them names from her family, Diane and David, Shane, Opal, and Eugene. She went back to Grandma Massey's name, Opal, and circled it again. She wrote it down in the notebook over and over, making the name thicker and bolder on the page. Then she circled her brother's name, Shane, and made it bold and drew a frame around it.

She boiled the last two eggs for supper that night. Bobo was on the couch, shaking. "Swarms," he said, and he slapped himself on his arms and legs, his jaw clenching and releasing. She peeled the eggs at the counter in the kitchen and ate them there, out of his sight, then sneaked to the bedroom and locked the door. The window was too high to climb out of, so she grabbed the laundry basket and turned it over, but when she stood on it, it crumpled. She kicked it out of the way and tried to push the bed over to the wall but it wouldn't budge. The doorknob shook. "What's going on in there?" Bobo said as he pounded the door.

"Just a minute," she said.

"If you don't open this—" and right as he said that Marie opened the door. He stood in his underwear, still slapping and digging at himself. His eye sockets were purple-black and his skull looked like it was fighting its way out of his skin. He didn't look real. He looked like a skull on top of a skeleton. He wasn't Bobo anymore.

"I'm done," she said and she walked by him in the doorway. He cussed her and followed her into the kitchen. She opened the refrigerator and every cabinet door, above and below. When all the doors were open, she turned to him. "There's not one thing left in this house to eat and if we don't have something soon, we're going to starve, me and the baby." He stood, not saying anything, scratching one arm with the other. "You don't even care about us," Marie said. "Just let us go."

He went to the living room and sat down on the couch. "Come in here. I been thinking about how we're going to work this all out." His legs were spread open and she thought he wanted a blow job, even though he'd hardly touched her since they found out she was pregnant. But then he put his legs together. "Go get some clothes on. We're going to go for a little drive."

Marie went to the bedroom and took off the stretchy pants from the dollar store and the XXL T-shirt she got from the tub of maternity clothes Crystal brought. She put them in the dirty clothes pile in the middle of the floor, then pulled a dress out from the bottom of the pile. It was wrinkled and it stunk a little like body odor, but it also smelled like the raspberry body lotion she had put on at Crystal's house. She put makeup on to cover the bruises on her face from Bobo hitting her with the flashlight.

Marie followed Bobo outside. She stood on the landing. Her eyes were swollen and she had to shield them from the sunlight.

She felt like she had been sick and was finally able to get up and around. She stepped down into the yard and Bobo grabbed her by the elbow and guided her to the passenger side. He drove downtown. He parked in front of the drugstore and told her the plan. She would go directly to the cold medicine aisle. He would cause a distraction and she would put three boxes of decongestant down in her purse, and they would walk out together. When they got out of the Jeep he took hold of her elbow again.

It was a small old-timey store. There was wood paneling on the walls, and a big wooden Rx symbol above the greeting cards. It was like having to go in the hardware store to buy lye all over again. Only this time it was women who worked the cash register at the back of the store watching the two of them.

Bobo guided Marie to the cold and allergy section, then let her elbow go and went back to the cashiers. "You all got any of that Tiger Balm?" he said, real loud. Marie heard the women ask him what it was. "It's from China or somewhere. Put it on your elbow, or whatever is hurting you." The cashiers talked about whether they had it, and if they did, where it could be in the store. Marie slipped the boxes of pills into her purse. One cashier came out from behind the counter and walked Bobo over to an aisle on the other side of the store and showed him the Bengay. "That's not what I'm after. This stuff has a tiger on it. It smells like cinnamon or something." Marie sneaked out the front door while Bobo was talking to the woman. She started walking fast down the sidewalk, away from Bobo's Jeep, not looking back.

She slipped into the auto parts store and headed to the back as fast as she could to hide. But Bobo had seen her and followed her in. He was beside her before she could get there. He took hold of her arm and turned to leave but Marie grabbed onto a shelf and stopped them.

"Just let me go, Bobo," she said, her voice getting louder. "You don't even want me anymore and you got the money back. I'll just go home and you can do whatever you want."

"Can I help you with something?" a man who worked there asked them. He stood at the end of the aisle, hands on his hips.

"Ah, we're good," Bobo said. "She wants some kind of air freshener, but I'm trying to tell her we don't have the money for it right now." They walked by the man and Marie tried to tell him what was wrong using her eyes and her face, but apparently she didn't do a good job because he let them walk on by.

Bobo opened the passenger side door. "Don't you even try that shit again." Marie got in and he slammed the door shut. He was mad but he drove her to the grocery store, then told her what was going to happen. He wasn't spending any money on her if she was going to act stupid, like what she just pulled. He made her put the medicine she took from the drugstore in the glove box, then dump everything from her purse onto the floorboard. Whatever food she could fit in her purse, she could have.

As soon as they went through the automatic doors of the store, Marie grabbed a buggy. Bobo jerked her arm, but he couldn't do anything since they were in public, so he held tight to the cart. She knew he had money on him and if they went through the checkout line, he'd have to pay. She pushed the cart down the aisles, he was cussing under his breath the whole time. She put milk and honey buns and cans of soup and cans of ravioli and peanut butter and crackers and spaghetti and bread and Coke in the cart. She could feel people looking at them. A mom in the cereal aisle pulled her little girl close to her so Marie and Bobo could pass them. "You think you're pretty smart," he said when they got back in the Jeep.

"No, I think I'm dumb," Marie said.

He nodded and lit a cigarette. "Yeah you are. And you're going to pay for messing with me."

"Just let me go. You want me gone anyway."

He shook his head. "Nope. I got plans for you."

When they got back to the house he made her bring all the groceries in. She started putting the food away and he put the pills in a bag in the hall closet. He pushed the couch up against the door again. If she hadn't been starving, she would have gone straight to the bedroom to get away from him, but she dumped a can of ravioli into a bowl and warmed it in the microwave. She poured herself a Coke. She took her supper to the bedroom and ate it on the bed. When she was finished, she propped herself up to help with the heartburn, and tried to sleep. She didn't bother to brush her teeth or take the dress off.

THE NEXT MORNING Bobo was sitting on the couch. He looked worse than the day before. He made her sit across from him in the chair. "Did you honestly think I would not miss fifteen hundred dollars? Look around you." Marie kept her eyes on the coffee table between them. "I'm serious. Look the fuck around you." She wouldn't move her head or her eyes, so he stood her up, grabbed her neck and moved her head, turned her in a circle around the room. "You aren't in the subdivision anymore." He let go of her neck but stayed next to her.

"But you've got the money back," Marie said. "You've got it."

"You're missing the point." He sat down on the couch and took a long draw on his cigarette. "Tell me something. What were you going to use it for? Maybe take a trip, go down to Mexico, Cancun or someplace your rich-ass family used to go."

"It was for the baby. Babies need things. Like cribs, which you destroyed. You don't even care."

He got up from the couch and walked away then. He came back with keys and the plastic grocery bag full of his supplies from the hallway closet. "Let's go," he said.

"Where?"

"All this we been talking about's going to get squared away. You're going to help me out on a batch. You been wanting to help, now you get to."

"I need to go to the bathroom." She stayed in there as long as she could.

Bobo was talking with someone in the living room. "You're here just in time," she heard him say. "You're going with us."

"I can't," the voice said. It was Nikki.

"Yeah," he said. "You're going. I got everything loaded."

Marie washed her hands and splashed water on her face. When she came into the living room, Nikki was in scrubs, one of the few times Marie had ever seen her in work clothes. And her hair didn't look right, it was like she had been sleeping on it and it was messed up in the back. She stood beside her brother and they were the same mess, in different bodies.

They got in the Jeep, Marie in the back seat, Bobo driving, Nikki in the passenger seat. They started down the road to Pennington. The road never changed, except what was blooming in the yards, depending on the season. Now the yards had greened up and people had Welcome Spring flags hanging from their porches. Marie noticed the car lot with used Fords, the roads with names like Upper Calloway and Pine Hill, in a way she hadn't before. The drive always meant they were going to do something, get on the river or work in the store. This time was different. Nikki sat silent looking out the window.

Marie imagined herself running away from Bobo, running down the street in Pennington, running fast even though she was pregnant, so fast she could not be stopped. Her feet wouldn't even touch the ground. She'd float fast over the sidewalk, pass over the old highway, see the river below her. She'd pass over the town of Crawford, on up the old highway to Caudill, where she'd stop at her parents' house. Her brother would be there and he would be so happy to see her. She'd eat pancakes and he'd eat bacon. They'd be alone in their floating eating-pan-cakes-and-bacon world. The two of them would be so happy that they'd glow, and other people would want to be with them because they'd be so beautiful and golden and happy. After a while the old true Bobo would join them, wearing his overalls and black T-shirt, his camo hat and sunglasses. He'd be the same Bobo Marie met by the bonfire. It would be the most amazing feeling, all of them together like that.

BOBO WAS TRYING to see the river as he drove, how it was running. He had the window down but it was hard to see through the new green on the trees. He craned his neck and wasn't looking at the road. He drifted across the line toward a car coming the other direction. "Bobo!" Nikki yelled. "Bobo!" Marie yelled. The other car honked and swerved out of the way.

He corrected the Jeep, corrected too much and the wheels hit the rumble strip and dropped off the shoulder completely. He didn't even try to get the wheels back up on the road. The Jeep went into the grass, hurtling toward a wall of rock that had been cut for the highway. Marie shrieked and so did Nikki. Bobo's hands and arms were like pink wires melted into the wheel, tendons and veins like cables. He finally got the Jeep stopped, or maybe a big rock stopped the wheels before they hit the wall.

Bobo hit the steering wheel with his hands, over and over. Finally Nikki said, "Stop it, Bobo," real soft, and he stopped.

236

Marie closed her eyes and everything was quiet. She could hear everyone breathing. They breathed in at the same time, breathed out at the same time. She unbuckled her seat belt and laid down across the back seat. Bobo put the Jeep in reverse, but it wouldn't budge. He put it in park and he and Nikki got out to look at the damage. Marie sat up and looked out the window.

Nikki got in and put the Jeep in reverse again, and Bobo pushed. The Jeep started to move backward, slowly at first, then Nikki gunned it, and Bobo stood there, helpless and alone, as they moved backwards away from him, cigarette in his mouth, but just barely because his mouth was open, his hands still out in front of him from pushing the Jeep.

Marie leaned up close to Nikki. "Go," Marie whispered. "Just keep going. Please!" Nikki turned the Jeep and pointed it back toward Crawford. She looked at her brother who was jogging toward them now. Marie thought Nikki was going to do it, to drive away, to leave him running there behind them, but then she put the Jeep in park. "We might as well get this bullshit over with," Nikki said without taking her eyes off her brother. She slid over to the passenger seat.

Marie threw the back door open and got into the driver's seat. She knew Bobo had seen her, knew he was moving faster now, but she didn't stop. She locked the door and moved to close the window but Bobo got his hand in and opened the door. He pulled Marie out of the seat and onto the ground. He stood over her and spit on the ground next to her.

"Come on," Nikki said, "she just wanted to drive. Don't make a fucking scene here by the side of the road, man."

Bobo looked down at Marie. "Get up," he said.

Marie pushed her hands down onto the gravel to get up. She stood and wiped the dirt off her hands.

"Get in the car right now."

"Just leave me here, Bobo. I'll find a way home."

"If I leave you here," he said, "I'll leave you here dead. Now get in before I bash your head in."

"If you morons don't get in right now, I'll bash both your heads in," Nikki said. "You're asking for the sheriff to show up."

Bobo pushed Marie into the back seat, got into the driver's side and locked the doors. He pulled the Jeep onto the highway, did a U-turn and headed to Pennington like nothing had happened. It was like they hadn't even stopped. It was like the road had always been there under them. Marie caught a flash of yellow on the side of the road as Bobo sped past the houses. Forsythia bushes, like a riot of yellow in someone's yard.

PENNINGTON was the same as always. The one restaurant in town was open. A couple of old men sat on a bench in front of the Main Street Mini-Mall that had closed down. They watched the Jeep pass by. Bobo pulled into a parking space on the street. Bert's blue BMW with the rusted hood was parked across the road. The store looked sad from the outside. The COMING SOON! OWENS OUTFITTERS! sign she had made and taped in the window hung down sideways in front of the yellowed newspapers. The storefront still needed to be painted. Marie had picked out the colors, but those paint chips had been lost long ago. The wood under the windows had rotted down close to the sidewalk, which was cracked and weedy in places.

The door to the store was open and Marie could hear a table saw and a radio going. Bert was inside, leaning over the saw, pencil behind his ear.

"What are you doing here?" Bobo yelled.

"Finishing up this framing," Bert said.

"Do you think it's a good idea to unload this stuff right here in the middle of town in broad daylight?" Nikki asked. Bobo scanned Main Street. The windows of one old building were boarded up. The thrift store was closed. The post office was closed. "Be all right," he said. "Time to make some cash."

They got the stuff out of the Jeep and carried it into the store. Bobo locked the door and they started setting up. He moved a sawhorse up toward the front of the room, and had Nikki move another one. He got an old door out of the back storage area and put it across the sawhorses to make a table. He told Marie to dump the water out of a cleaning bucket and wipe it dry. Nikki set up an electric burner and put a box of glass jars on the table.

Bert walked up next to Bobo. "Son, I don't believe you need to be doing that here." Bert nodded toward Marie. "And she's pregnant, she doesn't need to be around this stuff." But Bobo didn't seem to hear him.

"All right get over here," Bobo said to Marie. "What I'm going to show you is a throwdown batch. Quick and dirty." He took a package of gloves out of the cardboard box, the yellow kind people used to wash dishes with. He threw a plastic bag full of cold pills over to Bert. "Take all those out of the packages," he said. "Put them in that bucket there." He told Marie to help Bert.

Marie sat down in a metal folding chair beside Bert. He opened the boxes and took out the clear plastic bubble sheets. They started popping the red pills out through the foil back, letting them fall down into the bucket. The pills looked like Red Hots.

"I have to get out of here," Marie said under her breath without looking at Bert. She kept pushing the pills through the foil. Bert didn't look at her or say anything. He stayed leaned over, elbows on his knees. Nikki and Bobo were hard at work. Nikki was stirring something, straining it through a coffee filter into a jar.

239

"Do you think you can break that window in the front door?" Bert asked in a whisper. "You can use that stool up there."

Marie nodded.

Bert looked gray. Bobo had turned the burner on and something was bubbling in a glass jar. The fumes were heavy and toxic smelling. "I'm going to distract him and when I do, you run."

"What are you talking about over there?" Bobo yelled. "You all need to get to work. Stop your gabbing."

Bert took a box of cold pills and acted like he was opening it. He waited until Bobo was very intent on the stuff that was bubbling in front of him, then he ran up and kicked a leg of the sawhorse, which jarred and shook what they were working on. Bobo and Nikki both reached out and grabbed their jars. Bert kicked the sawhorse again, and some of the stuff sloshed out onto them, and they cussed and yelled, and that was Marie's chance. She ran to the front door, grabbed the stool and crashed it against the glass. She looked back just in time to see the flash of light and the pool of blue fire spreading across the floor, see Bobo's arms lit up and waving, Nikki's hair up in flames.

Bert was yelling *Go! Go! Go!* and trying to run after her. She got through the shattered door then a loud boom rocked the ground beneath her and the glass from the windows exploded out onto the sidewalk, the whole store now engulfed in flames. Marie held her arm up over her face to shield against the heat.

She hurried toward the restaurant. When she got inside, people were trying to figure out what had happened, what was going on. Marie asked if she could use their phone. "We don't allow anyone to use the phone," a woman said. She was looking out the window of the restaurant, down the street toward the store.

"I need to call 911 and the fire department and the ambulance," Marie said. "There are three people in there."

The woman looked at her, looked down at her belly. "Honey, the fire department's already been called. But if you need to call somebody else and it's not long distance, you can come on back."

Marie followed her around a corner to a phone mounted on the wall. She dialed the number. The phone rang three times. She heard her mother's voice say hello.

"Mom, I need you to come and get me. There's a fire and Bobo's dead and his sister and their friend. They're all dead."

It was quiet on the other side, quiet for a long time. Marie thought she could hear her mom breathing.

"Mom?"

"Yes. Tell me where you are. I'm leaving right now."

AS SHE WAITED for her mom, Marie walked back down Main Street toward the store. Fire was shooting out of the windows now, out of the roof. The building had partially collapsed.

She sat down by herself on the bench in front of the Mini-Mall. She put her hands between her belly and her breasts, and tried to breathe deep. She tried to breathe slow. "It's going to be okay, baby," she said. "It's going to be okay."

Pennington people came out of their houses to watch the fire. They looked at Marie, then back at the fire. She barely noticed them. She just watched the volunteer fire department send sprays of water onto the flames.

Acknowledgments

THIS BOOK would not have been written without the encouragement and support of many. My parents Nancy and Roland, siblings Callie and Mikhael, Dyche and Jenna, and all my nieces and nephews; Bobby, Jannette, Tiffany, Amy and Jonathan; Professors Pat White and Gurney Norman at the University of Kentucky, and Darnell Arnoult at Sweetwater, teachers who are as generous as they are genius; the Hell of Our Own writers, Wes Browne, Valetta Browne, Larry Thacker, Donna Crow, Sylvia Woods, Wendy Dinwiddie, Denton Loving, Tiffany Williams, and especially the real deal artist and fellow rover Robert Gipe; Berea writing buddies Angela Anderson, Christie Green, and especially Laura Nagle, a true writer and a true friend; Hindman teachers and friends including Lee Maynard, Ann Pancake, Glenn Taylor, Pam Duncan, C. Michael Curtis, Jenny Barton, Sandy Ballard, Jim Minnick and Mike Mullins. Thanks to editors Donna Sparkman, George Brosi, Charles White, Marianne Worthington, Silas House, Jason Howard, Savannah Sipple and Elizabeth McKenzie, who published short stories and excerpts. Special thanks to Nyoka Hawkins and Old Cove Press for bringing this book into print. Thank you grandma Hattie Roosevelt Morris Mullins who said I could, and daughters Aden and Lydia who inspire me every day. Special thanks to my husband Bob who has always believed even when it wasn't easy, and who is the reason this ever got done, thank you for that, and for everything.

Publisher's Note

OLD COVE PRESS thanks Sharon Hatfield and Stephanie Adams for expert editorial assistance. Thanks also to Battalion Chief Joe Best of the Lexington Fire Department for technical advice. Special thanks to actress Savannah Adams for expanding our understanding of the characters and the story.

Author

CARRIE MULLINS grew up in Mt. Vernon, Kentucky, where she still lives. *Night Garden* is her first novel.